QUEEN
OF THE
SUGARHOUSE

Books by Constance Studer:

Prayer To A Purple God,
Mellen Poetry Press

Body Language: First Of All Do No Harm,
Purdue University Press

QUEEN
OF THE
SUGARHOUSE

Stories by
Constance Studer

atmosphere press

For my son, Christopher,
with gratitude for your encouragement.

TABLE OF CONTENTS

Mercy ~ 3

Shelter ~ 22

Think Beauty ~ 38

This Middle Kingdom ~ 59

Shift ~ 77

The Isolation Room ~ 95

Testament ~ 113

Special Needs ~ 122

Queen of the Sugarhouse ~ 138

"There are two mountains on which the weather is bright and clear, the mountain of the animals and the mountain of the gods.

But between lies the shadowy realm of men."

-- Paul Klee,
Diaries 1898-1918

MERCY

My car threw a hub cap on my drive to work. There are police in the parking lot as I pull into my spot. "Here, I'll walk you in," the cop says, one hand on his gun.

Pick any day and stand by the ER door and you can see a frail man, unquestionably end-stage AIDS, or a woman holding a washcloth to her sliced finger. A prisoner from county jail with a bloody face, bruised chest, hands and ankles cuffed. Mothers with their restless children in tow looking ill at ease because they've lost their insurance.

Streets around our hospital are always teeming. Nurses and techs have a smoke and a giggle in August sun. Proud new mothers in oversized clothes bear small bundles to waiting cars. There's a small-town campus feel to our hospital, jazzed and vibrant, energizing and disturbing. Security guards and doctors and nurses struggle to control the comings and goings of patients who shout the mantra, *"It hurts, oh it hurts."*

Up to the locker room. Loose-fitting white pants, white

socks, white sneakers. Pink and blue T-shirt completes my ensemble. I close my locker door, clip my ID badge to my shirt. Past doors marked *Radiology, Pathology, Nuclear Medicine.* Then I swing through the doors of the ICU, this never-never land where instruments vie for dominance over people. With a twirl of my swivel chair, I pour a cup of coffee and listen to the taped report, pen in hand, taking notes on my patients. *Tanya Lewis was depressed and crying part of the night...* I listen until the tape ends.

Working short-staffed again. Endless interruptions. Phone calls. Lab tests. IVs to be changed. Sterile dressings. Head-to-toe assessments. I'm passing nine o'clock meds and the minute that Tanya Lewis swallows, I realize that I just handed her the wrong pill. She is one of three patients I'm taking care of this Thursday. There had been six little white cups on the tray. My hand had reached for the wrong one. Phones ring constantly. Computer screens glow with facts and figures. Doors open, close. Air hums with running feet, a high-tech symphony of beeps and buzzers.

Heat in an Intensive Care is amniotic. Tanya huddles in the corner of her bed, her anxious eyes dart from my hand holding her glass of water to the clock on the wall. "My husband is waiting outside. Will you let him in?" Sweat rolls down her forehead. Her heart rate is too rapid. A thin green tube forces oxygen into her nose. Her breath is short gasps. Wires under her gown tether her to the bedside monitor that chirps each erratic beat of her weakened heart.

I retreat to the med room, lean my head against the wall, close my eyes. All I want is to fold in on myself, to float in an ocean of silence. All around telephones ring. Dr.

4

Bryan yells for a chart. Hands shaking, I walk to the waiting room where Tanya's husband has set up camp. He slept in the waiting room last night so he could see his wife for fifteen minutes every two hours.

"You may go in now, Bill," I say, holding the door open for him. He is tall, probably mid-forties, with brown hair thinning at the crown. His face is all angles and planes, a face a sculptor could do something with. His grey suit is wrinkled, his eyes tense with worry. He gathers up the briefcase that he was using as a pillow and hurries past me to his wife's bedside. He leans down to kiss her on the lips and Tanya's face becomes radiant at the sight of him. "Are you all right?" they both say at the same moment, then laugh. Bill sits on the edge of her bed, stroking her hair with his hand.

Maybe love is a gift given only to certain people, like perfect pitch or the ability to draw.

And as if in slow motion, over and over in my mind I'm holding out Tanya's glass of water, watching as she draws up on the straw, swallows a pill not meant for her. No time for rules of passing medications: right drug, right time, right dose, right method of administration, right patient. Too late to take back my mistake. I've made my heart a desert and call it peace.

On my days off, I used to forget about all the wounds I've seen by dancing at the Grizzly Rose. It was Friday night five years ago that I met him. The dance floor was hip-to-hip with men and women dressed in jeans and t-shirts and tank tops. Paulo had everyone's attention under the dazzle of strobe lights. Shoulder-length black hair swayed with each movement of his head, his body fluid against the harsh beat of the guitar. He spun, one hand waving free. All eyes were on him.

"Come dance," he said, holding out his hand, pulling me onto the floor. He grabbed me around the waist and twirled me hard, pushed my body against his. He flirted, played with my hair, touched my waist, my arms. Paulo was big with well-defined muscles, but he told me his history in the strength of his hands: *I was born in the mountains of Costa Rica… my family traveled six weeks to get to the States.* Always there was a sadness hovering behind his eyes. Sex was the one thing I'd gotten behind on the most and thought I could catch up on the quickest. Better than aspirin for what ailed me.

In ICU, lights are never turned off. In this windowless place, it's always now. Sensory and stimuli-deprived patients lapse into confusion, ICU psychosis, floating in a haze of medication, pain, fear. The unit has six curtained cubicles, plus a glass-enclosed isolation room clustered around the nurses' station. Five rooms for coronary patients complete the other half of the circle. Each room has a monitor overhead for EKG readings, arterial lines, intracranial pressure readings. Suction equipment, blood pressure device, rubbery IV bags with tubing snaking through machines that count each drop. Nitro drip for pain control, antibiotic drip, straight-in or piggy-backed.

Alarms keep watch over everything. *Something is wrong.* Ventilators beep when interrupted for suctioning and honk for pulmonary pressure changes. Patients long for the human touch of a bath, a walk, a conversation. No one thanks a nurse for flushing his central line. Monitors bong if a blood pressure is too high or too low. Even the beds are smart.

"Can I talk to you, Ann? Please?" Bill Lewis asks. I'm barreling through the unit with a load of clean linen in my right hand and a bottle of Dextrose and Water in my left. It's his hand on my arm that brings me to a halt.

"What can you tell me about Tanya's condition?" His smile is thin and tight.

"Her heart rate is still too fast. She's still running a significant fever, which is what has us worried." Tanya has MS. As if that weren't enough, she also received a new mitral valve last month. Now, because of her increased risk of infections, we're watching her closely.

"Thank you. That's what I wanted to know. I'll be here if you need me," Bill says as he half bows out of the room. Through the glass door I watch him carefully remove his suit jacket, place it on the chair next to the sofa, settle in for a long wait.

I hurry on. Pass meds. Hang IV. Transcribe orders. Constantly, we play the game of musical beds. Who is the sickest? Who can we move to make room for the gunshot wound in ER? Who can I bump over to the wards? So many times I've seen the signs of imminent death: a blurring of the body's boundaries, a gentle and sometimes not-so-gentle fusion with surrounding elements, a sigh into oblivion.

Someone has died on our unit every shift for a week. Monday it was Mrs. Tomlin, a woman with DIC, a bleeding disorder, Lucy's patient, who, it turns out, received the wrong blood. She bled out and died and no one wanted to do CPR, no one wanted their name on her chart because her husband swears he'll sue. Blood is a smell the brain never forgets, a smell that goes straight to some deep, primitive center of the cortex. We had a meeting to discuss the circumstances around her death: *Did I do the right thing? Could I have done something different to change the situation?*

A thirty-year-old waitress shot herself and died four days later, her face caved in. Tiny glinting pieces of human brain tissue mixed with crimson splatters. Lance, an eighteen-year-old, was admitted for a hernia repair and went into cardiac arrest on the OR table. He is one of my patients today too. Brain-stem dysfunction. No pupillary light reflex, no gag reflex, no spontaneous respirations. *Dolls' eyes response*, the neurologist wrote on his chart. As I bathe him, the room is filled with the rhythmic sound of the respirator, its small protective glass cage misted with condensation, its black balloon collapsing and refilling, inhaling and exhaling, making its fist and opening to its blossom, over and over again. Lucy and Carol fly by on their way to their own private emergencies, their faces full of determination. Nothing we do is ever enough.

Paulo was eight years younger. We had an immediate understanding. I never had to explain my life to him. Paulo, splendid in his white linen suit, dark limpid eyes. Romantic without being controlling. After all my one-night stands, I believed romance was a patriarchal plot to hide women behind thick walls and to hook us into bearing lots of male children. I'd fallen in love about once a month before I met Paulo. Sex, that weaving dance of give and take, the swirling of minds, the dip and sway of dreams, dance of the senses. All of a sudden I wasn't looking over his left shoulder wondering about the next encounter with someone else.

Paulo won me over with his hands. We were in the shower, soaping each other's backs. Peppermint soap, the smell, the tingling. We slid around on each other's skin and morning sun shone into the shower through the hanging plants. Water sparkled on our bodies as we bathed. And all at once, we were in a jungle waterfall cavorting among vines and rocks. Wild animals.

We began to growl and paw each other's bodies. I grabbed Paulo and started to lick him all over, from the bottom of his backbone, moving up his spine. *Tiger woman*, he called me. *Tiger man*, I growled back.

We stepped out of the shower and shook water out of our hair, rolled our bodies dry on big shaggy towels. We moved from bedroom to living room to kitchen, licking each other. The bed was our cave. No boundaries. Not an inch, inside or out, that we didn't explore. What is love but imagination that gives, takes, breathes, and has room, like skin, to expand?

Tanya lies in bed, talking to her husband. She looks OK. Is it a mistake only if I get caught? The unit is quiet, almost becalmed. I sit with Lucy and Carol in the nurses' station, our island comprised of two long desks equipped with computers and phones and monitors. Dr. Logan, Tanya's doctor, walks in. He is the one I must tell.

"Do you have a minute?"

"Only one," he says, following me into the conference room. I shut the door.

"I gave Tanya Lewis Lanoxin instead of Lasix this morning. I'll make out an incident report." Lanoxin is a form of digitalis and is given to slow and strengthen the heartbeat. Lasix helps remove excess fluid.

"Is this the first time you've ever given someone the wrong medicine?" Dr. Logan asks in his I'm-the-doctor-you're-the-peon tone of voice. His skin is the color of ash.

"As far as I know. I knew the moment I saw her swallow the pill. I feel terrible."

"Don't tell anyone. No sense asking for a lawsuit," he says. I look at him in amazement, then remember to whom I'm speaking. This is the doctor who wrote an order for 50 milligrams Demerol to be given intravenously to Sylvia, one of our patients admitted in respiratory distress. She was coughing up bright red blood from ravaged lungs. Ventilator. Twenty-one years old.

Sick for two weeks with "flu." I knew he must mean IM instead. Fifty milligrams of Demerol intravenously would kill her. I called him and pointed out his error and asked him to change the order. He flew into a rage.

"How could you question my order?" he had yelled. I called Barbara, our head nurse, who called Dr. Logan and explained the situation in her most diplomatic style. He told her to go to hell. He threatened to have her fired. *Give the drug as ordered*, he insisted.

As a last resort, Barbara called the Chief of Medicine at home. He put a hold on Dr. Logan's order instead of canceling it, refused to prescribe another analgesic to take its place. Sylvia went without pain medication for over twenty-four hours because her doctor wouldn't admit he'd made a mistake.

"Doctor, you haven't heard a word I've said," I say as I rise to leave. When does memory stop being blame?

I keep finding excuses to check on Tanya. She's laughing with her husband. "So how are you feeling?" I ask as I adjust the drops-per-minute on her IVAC. Her heart rate on the monitor is slower, more regular.

"I'm better now that Bill is here," Tanya says. She's breathing more easily. Her skin is dry. Maybe her fever has finally broken. Bill runs a brush through her long brown hair.

"Isn't she beautiful?" Bill says.

"Quit," Tanya says, but her eyes say, *Tell me more.*

"This isn't a beauty contest," I say.

"Good thing," Tanya laughs. I exit around the curtain as Tanya lays her head on Bill's chest and he rubs her back. Standing there watching them, I'm jealous how in love they are. Wanting to be wanted. Listened to. Really listened to, the way Paulo listened to me. I could say anything, *I bought peas for dinner* or *my car needs an oil change.* It was the way he looked at me when I talked. Suddenly I wasn't talking about my car anymore. I was revealing everything I ever knew about myself. The girls I used to jump rope with, the tree I laid under as a child, my first kiss. The way I pushed my hair back from my forehead, knitted my brow, tightened my lips when I was trying to remember a name. Love was a sudden look of appreciation. He noticed everything, so I dressed for him, bathed for him, put on perfume and makeup. I felt known. No longer just one woman in the multitude. I was unique. Me. That was what it felt like to be loved.

When I go to the utility room to empty a urine bag, I feel dizzy and think I'm going to pass out. No lunch. All I can see is Tanya with her eyes rolling back into her head and her monitor straight-lining and me pushing the COR O button and putting the head of Tanya's bed down, giving her quick breaths, starting chest compressions. COR O the paging system shouts. Feet run. The team crowds around her bed. Her gown slips down revealing her chest.

Commotion escalates. She's in V-fib. Death, the great equalizer, the great surprise.

"Are you all right?" Lucy asks as she watches me peeking through the door. Tanya is mulling her choices on the menu. Bill is changing the music on her CD player, helping her put the earphones back on.

"No. I'm not," I say.

"Anything I can do?" Lucy asks as she pushes her curly hair behind her ears.

"It's something I've got to work out for myself." Other scenes pass before my eyes: Standing in front of the Director of Nursing as she tells me I'm fired. Being hauled before the State Nursing Board—*Your nursing license has been revoked.* Slinging hash at Salinger's Diner.

Colorado air is always in motion, sometimes a chinook blast, sometimes a gentle January whisper. A hushabye soughing of pinons nearby. Paulo had a little cabin by Grand Lake. It was about ten degrees when I got there. Snow squeaked under my heels. The hairs in my nostrils vibrated like wind chimes. The cabin was one room with an old black and silver potbellied stove in the center. When I opened the door, heat drew me in. He had lit candles on the table and soup was simmering on the stove. The smell of beef and carrots and onions, such comfort. After all those years of tension and taking care of everyone else in the universe, I couldn't say a word.

Paulo reached out for my hand and led me to the mattress on the floor and said, "Let me give you a massage." I accepted and he gently stripped me before I could think. I was lying on Paulo's bed, naked, with my arms plastered to my sides. My stomach was tense. I laid there with my eyes shut and heard him stoke the stove and put a bottle of massage oil to warm in a pan of water. Then he moved behind me on the mattress, slid his back against the wall and straddled my body. He placed his big, incredibly warm hands under my neck. He held them there and leaned over and whispered in my ear, "Remember to breathe."

His breath was like sweet grass. "Listen for my breathing and then breathe along with me," I forced myself to take in air and expel it so I'd at least look like I was alive. Then he sat up and poured warm oil into his palms. The room filled up with a healing smell I remembered from childhood. The kind that clears out your sinuses in a whiff.

He slid his hands down my shoulders and arms and, in the same motion, pulled me up from the waist, lifted my body and spread my ribcage so that I finally did begin to breathe, gulping in air down to my toes. I opened my eyes and looked up at him, into that strong-boned, upside-down face. The whites of his eyes were so clear they were almost blue.

"What are you doing?" I whispered.

"I'm showing you how love feels," he said. There seemed to be less and less space between us, as if we were becoming one rhythm. His hands found my stomach. He drizzled warm oil into my belly button, drew a line up my body from belly, ever so slowly, to my throat and chin and nose and forehead, solemn, deliberate, like an initiation ceremony. He slid his body on top of mine, bellies touching, warm breath in each other's ears. A cry came from my mouth that would have awakened wolves or coyotes if there had been any left in the woods.

"Go grab some lunch," Lucy says. "I'll cover your patients. I'm worried about you," Our last admission, a transfer from a surgical floor, has settled in. The nurses' station is empty of doctors. The orders on the charts have been transcribed and hung back in their slots.

"Keep an eye on Tanya Lewis, okay?" Lucy shoos me off with a wave of her hand as she flies through the nurses' station on her way to answer a light.

Down the elevator, the cafeteria is a cave carved out in the basement. The smell is of too many burned pans of macaroni and cheese. I grab a tray and force my mind to decide between rigid spaghetti and limp salad. I settle for chicken-and-noodle soup.

"Come sit with me," Bill says. He has a full tray of spaghetti drowned in parmesan cheese, garlic bread.

"How can you look so good after being here so many hours, Bill?"

"As long as I'm near Tanya, I'm okay," he says as he makes room for me at his table. I fall into the seat. Only now do I feel how tired my muscles are.

"Have you and Tanya been married long?"

"Five years. I met her at a pottery show. She was selling her work. All I saw was her gorgeous smile and blue eyes. Then her wheelchair. It was her incredible spirit that I fell in love with. But it's still hard sometimes," Bill says, setting down his fork, his eyes clouded by worry. "Her MS is our illness. When do you think she'll be able to move out of ICU?"

"Soon. I think." I pick my words carefully. Hot soup

scalds my tongue.

COR O ICU COR O ICU the PA system blares. Bill and I look at each other then run for the stairs. *Please Lord don't let it be Tanya,* I pray. When I race into the unit, the new admit from the surgical floor is in full cardiac arrest. Lucy is on top of the bed doing chest compressions.

Carol is breathing for him, using an ambu bag. The ER doctor is talking with the attending. They call the code: *time of death, 2:46 p.m.* It's not Tanya. Grief is a train that doesn't run on anyone else's schedule. Medicine tries to turn grief into a set of rules, stages, deadlines; tuck messy emotions under neat clinical labels. Trauma. Pain. Detachment. Acceptance. Time's up. But there are no one-hour or one-year mourners.

The wife and daughter come and Lucy leads them behind the beige curtain where their loved one lies. They emerge a half-hour later wiping their eyes, bearing his belongings in a plastic bag. Mother and daughter lean against each other, like braces of a house. One wrong move by either of them and their support will cave in. Watching them, my heart aches and my throat almost shuts. Over and over I've witnessed grief, the breath checked and the heart belabored, the eyes giving up their tears, the tongue bitter as if it had tasted poison.

Voices float in from the corridor. Someone laughs. Trays litter bedside tables. IVACs pump like heartbeats. All around me swirl life and death issues. Mrs. Lanowski— long history of diabetes, admitted with gas gangrene of her right leg—has lapsed into total body failure: lungs, liver, kidney.

I turn her onto her right side, put a pillow behind her back, between her legs, carefully, as if the fragile bones might snap. Her feet are purple and cold to the touch. In the cubicle next to her is Larry Thompson, an eighteen-year-old boy whose brain is gone because he refused to wear a motorcycle helmet. They lie side-by-side, facing opposite directions, like angry lovers.

In the past six months, three nurses from our unit have resigned. Last weekend Barbara threw a party for Marie. From the jukebox, Joni Mitchell was singing, *At last... my love has come along....* Margaritas flowed like tap water, the table heavy with homemade bread and pecan pie and fried chicken and ambrosia salad. I lounged on the floor next to the guest of honor.

"Did you hear the latest? They want to do mastectomies on an outpatient basis, amputate and out," Carol said as she licked chicken from her fingers.

"Lord help us. A woman goes into surgery anxious about life and death and mutilation. She comes out with not only pain and tubes but also psychological trauma. And they want to do drive-through mastectomies," Lucy said.

"I wonder exactly what part of a man's anatomy they'd amputate in same-day surgery?" Carol asked. "So, aren't you going to miss all this fun when you're selling real estate, Marie?"

"The last month of nights almost did me in."

"Give her a year and she'll be back," Lucy said. "She'll miss all the great food at our parties."

"Don't count on it. Too few nurses. Not enough money. Sicker patients. Who cares anyway? Where are the raised voices coming over radio waves and TV screens and newsstand headlines? If no one else cares, why should we?" Marie said. She sprang to her feet and waved her empty margarita glass in the air like a flag of surrender.

We had an August wedding by Grand Lake. Paulo in white cotton pants and flowing shirt, me in a long white cotton skirt and peasant blouse, which I wore off my shoulders. Baby white roses woven into my long brown braids. Friends formed a circle around us as we took turns saying our vows. *I promise to realize my full potential for both closeness and autonomy, to hold nothing back, to tell the truth, to listen non-judgmentally to what you say. I am responsible for my own happiness, well-being, life-goals.... I love you as you are this moment....*

We danced and sang along with a live band. For Paulo, romance was much more than a bouquet of roses. The day we married, Paulo brought me a Tibetan singing bowl that glowed with the softness and sheen of silk.

"This bowl was crafted in the high mountains from seven holy metals," he explained. "I see this bowl as a symbol for you, the woman I love. You are strong, like this bowl, round, with no corners or projectiles. Powerful like an open hand, not a closed fist. Listen," he said as he began to stroke the rim with a wooden dowel. He had a true sense of ceremony. The bowl was simple with no decoration but had a voice that opened the heart. We breathed together and listened until the sound reached our bones. It was a barely audible contralto, yet vibrant enough to waffle the eardrums, wring tears from my eyes. A voice of heartbeat, the hum earth sings.

There is a constant shuffle of patients. Every time an alarm goes off, Carol and Lucy or I race to see whose patient is in trouble. Eyeballing monitors, as I race through the nurses' station with a load of linen or an IV to be hung, is second nature. At its best, ICU is the finest medicine has to offer, swift intervention to save a life. At its worst, it's not so much life preserved as death prolonged.

I feel a fluttery touch on my back. It's the daughter of a woman who was transferred in from 4 North with a high fever. Probably sepsis.

"Please. Get my mother something for pain," her daughter pleads. I leaf through her chart and read the pathology report: Liver Cancer. Dorothy Simms is all bone and eyes and yellow skin. I search the med sheet for the time and amount of her last dose of pain medicine. I scan the nurses' notes and see *patient requesting pain medicine. Dr. Solano called for order. Order refused.*

"Why hasn't your mother been receiving pain meds?" I ask.

"I don't know what to do," the daughter says as she stands there twisting the edge of her sweater between white fingers.

"The physician is working with you and your mother, and you have the right to be part of the decision-making team," I say, reaching for the phone. I call and am put on hold, wait, then listen as Dr. Solano tells me that Dorothy has been trying to get narcotics from day one.

"I'll be in to see her," he says as the phone clicks.

"But she has cancer," I say to the dead phone. "Sorry. Dr. Solano is coming in. I can't do anything until he gets here." The daughter lowers her eyes, all guilty humility. She retreats to sit beside her mother's bed. There is no Book of Right Answers. All I can think about is whether or not I should tell Tanya Lewis about my mistake.

Just last week, before Paulo went to visit his brother in Costa Rica, I helped him strip the apple trees before the season's first snow could shock the fruits into mush. The glossiest apples graced a white bowl. For Paulo, cooking was instinctual, his movements quick and sure. *About this much flour*, he'd say, tapping the bowl. *And a handful of sugar*. It was the warmth of his hands that did it in the end, pressing and kneading. Cooking, like nursing, is all about hands, ladling out, putting in, touching. Hands will always be needed. Paulo's dumplings glimmer in the depths of my freezer, waiting to be discovered on a bitter-cold winter night, pale doughy globes with summer in their hearts.

"Are you ready for your bath?" I ask. Tanya lies peacefully reading a book. She looks better than she has for days. Her skin glows. Maybe the Lanoxin did her some good, or maybe that's just wishful thinking. Maybe it was seeing her husband. There is a hand-thrown pottery bowl on her bedside table.

"I'm ready if you are," Tanya says with a smile. I fill the basin with warm soapy water, gather her towel and washcloth, lower the head of her bed. "My husband told me to tell you that he appreciates how you keep him informed about my condition. He has a hard time reaching Dr. Logan."

"Did Bill bring the bowl?" I ask as I wash Tanya's right arm, up and back, then dry it with a towel. Tanya reads the expression on my face.

"I know, I know, I can't keep it in ICU, but yes it's one of mine. Bill wants me home fast and he knows the best way is to remind me of my passion. There's nothing like the feel of clay as I form it by hand on the potter's wheel. Days fly by when I'm wedging clay, rolling, paddling, coiling it to get out the air. When I get into the rhythm, it's like meditation."

"Is it hard to learn?" I drape her legs with the bath blanket. Both legs are withered, muscles atrophied. But her arm muscles are hard and well-defined by years of rolling along in her wheelchair.

"The trickiest part is putting the pot into the first fire, the bisque, embedding it in sawdust, firing it, letting it go to the elements, wind, rain, snow, whatever comes along. I never know what I'm going to end up with. It's when the pots crack in two in the kiln that I learn the most."

"It's a beautiful bowl. My husband loved pottery. He gave me a singing bowl once." Done with her legs, I start to wash her back. Through the curtain, I can hear Lucy's voice as she tapes her report for the evening nurses, her voice slow and tired, a kind of choral sigh.

I pull up a chair beside Tanya's bed and open my mouth to tell her about my mistake and hear Dr. Solano in the nurses' station yelling at Carol and think of Paulo lost in Costa Rica, no one knows where. About the flood that wiped out the village where his brother lived. My silence is the grief of not knowing whether Paulo is still alive, of trying to forgive myself for all my mistakes, a prayer for mercy. At night when I can't sleep, I run my finger around the rim of the singing bowl and hear Paulo's voice saying *relax, breathe, feel, let go of control. Be open to the outcome. My spirit is here in this room.* No healing comes without cost. Harm happens. No one is immune.

SHELTER

Everything I own is in the knapsack on my back. Cars pass full of folks dressed for church, spreading a cloud of gray dust that washes into my nose, setting off a fit of sneezing. Pale clouds change shape, colliding softly as the sun gains height. Even though it's January, the day is a breezeless sixty degrees. People are out walking their dogs, chatting with neighbors, closing drug deals on the corner.

There's a man far down the block with a bald scalp who reminds me of my father, who hustled me into a jacket over my cowboy pajamas, dug out tennis shoes from under a heap of clothes in the closet. "Hurry, or we'll miss it," Dad had said as he pulled me down the stairs into the backyard to watch Sputnik sprint across the sky. As we sat on wet grass, Dad snapped off the flashlight and pointed towards a faraway glimmer.

"This proves that men are the masters, Ben," my father told me. "It's up to your generation to save not only the Earth but outer space as well from the enemy."

"Who is the enemy?" I asked.

"Anyone who tries to push us around," he said. My father was a man so tall he had to duck through doorways. At first, all I could see was a blanket of stars spread out between trees. Finally, I saw a pinpoint of light crawling across the sky, so powerful, yet so fragile.

I grew up high in the San Juan mountains of Colorado, a landscape where gold and silver were long ago scratched out of the mountains I call home.

"I lived off rabbits during the Depression," my father told me, "the price of a bullet cost so much. I couldn't afford to miss. I became a damn good shot."

Ouray is an old mining town that has suffered since the silver mines were shut down after my father came back from Nam. The isolation of living in the mountains can be intense. I was raised on my mother's stories, how she came to Ouray to become the only teacher in the simple one-room schoolhouse. All the years she spent hauling water and searching riverbeds for coal in order to keep our house warm. Everything I know I learned from her, how to recite poems by Longfellow and the multiplication tables and the Pledge of Allegiance.

I haul a sack of cans to the store and have just enough money for bus fare to the VA Hospital. On the way up to see the doctor, I stop in to check on my permanent disability claim.

"What name is the claim under?" the woman behind the desk asks. "Benjamin Tyler."

"That claim has been denied. We sent you a letter a

month ago."

"I didn't receive it. I'm living in shelters because you folks can't get it together," I shout. I can feel my face contort.

The woman puts her chair between us. "You'll have to fill out another application. Your doctors will have to resubmit their documentation of your disability." She extends a sheaf of papers. It takes all the concentration I can muster for me to still the trembling in my arms enough so that I can grab the folder.

I was helping my father on a construction site the day I told him that I'd signed up for Desert Storm. Each time Dad sliced off the end of a two-by-ten, a whiff of Big Woods came out. My father never was one for talking, but when he picked up a hammer, he was eloquent. He leaned forward and pursed his lips as if he were listening to the wood. His hammer sang as we put the final shingles on the roof, as a house emerged from its skeleton of architectural design, with its log siding, view of towering mountains, the lake.

I go up the hospital elevator for my appointment with the VA doctor. Each week I get sent to a different specialist, neurologist, hematologist, urologist, as different parts of my body exhibit alarming symptoms. Today my appointment is with Dr. Langell, an Immunologist. The doctor who investigates why a person's body turns on itself, cells fighting cells. I sit in the waiting room, settling into the pain. Inside the hospital, it's all stippled ceilings and vertical blinds, an antiseptic could-be-anywhere aesthetic.

"Benjamin Tyler? The doctor will see you now," a woman in green scrubs says. "What happened to your little finger?" The doctor asks, holding up my right hand.

"When I was a kid, I blew off the tip of my pinkie trying to ignite a miniature rocket in the back yard. I thought I was Superman, certain that I could fly. But all these tremors started after I got back from Desert Storm," I slowly explain to Dr. Langell, "it was all that stuff we were breathing. Or maybe something in the shots they gave us, I don't know. Here's a list of the shots I received," retrieving a crumpled paper from my knapsack. Vaccines. Smallpox. Anthrax.

"Nothing unusual here. Standard Military Protocol," Dr. Langell says. He has a walrus mustache and an auburn ponytail. Something yet unnamed is causing me to twitch and stumble and stutter. "I don't know what I can do for you," he says as he washes his hands at the sink.

"And there were chemical exposures," I insist as if the doctor hadn't spoken. "Oil smoke. Burnt tires. All I know is I've been to the Gulf War and I've been blowing gaskets ever since. And to think I actually volunteered for this misery." I gather my coat and knapsack, and head for the door.

Your father was drafted, my mother told me long after he became absent from my life. *He was never the same after his tour in Vietnam.* What did I know about going to war, me, part of a generation weaned on Hammer's rap music and Bart Simpson's impertinence? We landed on foreign soil with our Nintendo games and Instamatic cameras, all the while red sun blazed over desert sand. Shirt glued to plastic seat, I rode in a convoy across the desert not far from the Kuwaiti border. I lined up with my fellow soldiers, our all-volunteer force, for my shots, not knowing what they were for.

"What happens if I refuse?" I ask. No one answers.

This is not the game I used to play with my buddies when we were eleven and took turns being generals and attacking imaginary targets with dirt bombs. Back then I thought war was victory parades on D-Day and medals for a job well done. Now the battlefield was vast stretches of desert that looked like a giant garbage dump strewn with rusty automobile carcasses, deflated rubber tires and abandoned refrigerators, castoffs left to be consumed by sand and sun. Gas vents flamed bright orange. The only vegetation was salt brush that even camels couldn't stomach. The only sound was radio transmissions from inside the command vehicle.

"Red One. There are two vehicles up ahead. Tell me what you see." Grunts on the ground lived like animals, putting our lives on the line twenty-four hours a day, seven days a week, while our commanding officer was safe high above. An eye in the sky. Poor kids, black and chicano and white from small American towns awoke each morning to mortar rounds and the moans of our buddies crying out for a medic. Poor boys have always fought wars, those on the social fringe, oddballs who fall through the social cracks, unfortunates, those of us who work with our hands.

Stripping down to my fatigues, I tried to dig a foxhole like my CO instructed, but for every shovelful of sand I tossed out, three more sifted in. There were never enough sandbags to build a proper foxhole. Somehow, I learned to construct a small shelter with what was available, plywood or roots or scrub brush. And always I was homesick for the wood I used to lift up to my father. When I complained about how my hands were sticky from the pitch of lodgepole pines, he said, "Your hands get sticky to remind you that wood comes from something living."

Over weeks and months, I almost got used to being covered with the grit and grease of living on tanks for weeks and months without a shower, living with insects that looked like ladybugs but delivered a vicious bite. Cramped into the small foxhole at night, a raw chill swept across my damp skin. Obediently I gulped down the white pill that was supposed to protect me from nerve gas. We troops spread diesel oil on desert roads to control the dust as the sky spit oily raindrops.

Chemical weapons' alarms sounded. "False alarm," my commanding officer said. A SCUD missile came in. Kaboom. I was unloading the jeep when I heard the roar of a helicopter. As I turned, the craft exploded in midair, came apart before my eyes, tumbled to the ground. I was the nearest person to the crash, heard the rolling and thumping of metal, the cries of the men inside. I lunged forward and then stopped. The helicopter was in flames.

"Cease fire. Cease fire," a voice boomed. "We've shot down our own guys," a voice behind me whispered.

It is still five hours before the shelter opens when the sky spits rain and the temperature drops so low that I can see my breath. Just when I think I can't walk one block farther, I come across an abandoned bus with broken headlights and windows covered with cardboard, no tires or wheels even. It looks as if it had been dropped from a great height into the middle of the rest of the junk. I knock to see if this choice piece of real estate is taken. Someone has painted peace signs and hippie flowers and Deadhead slogans on the sides and it stinks pretty bad when the door is shut. The passenger seats are gone. The enclosure is surprisingly large. Two mattresses on the floor, a moldy sleeping bag, an aluminum chair and a table made from boards and bricks. On the ceiling is a poster from a Grateful Dead concert.

Making myself as comfortable as I can on the chair, I open a can of beer that I find in a cooler. I curl up in the sleeping bag and dream that I've fixed the bus up like a home and am tooling around America, stopping whenever and wherever I want, then taking off again, completely in charge of my life, carrying my shelter around with me, like pioneers in their covered wagons. *Going against the grain is a mistake,* I hear Dad say.

I'm awakened by a rough hand pulling me out of the sleeping bag. Rays of light stream through the cardboard. A tall man with ratty brown hair and a head shaped like a shovel towers over me as my eyes lock onto that hand with a tattoo: *Satan Lives.*

"Listen, you little shit, this is my house. Go find your own somewheres else," the man yells. I start twitching and my body jerks forward and the man is so startled that he lets me go without further trouble. Finding today's meal or bed or beer takes all my energy, leaving me nothing left over for thinking about next week. I am a veteran and can no longer vote because I have no home.

I'd never thought much about my body until I returned from Desert Storm. My semen started burning when Tillie and I made love. I slept poorly, nodded off behind the wheel of my truck. My legs balked at climbing the ladder at the construction site. Out of nowhere rashes sprouted

27

on chest, arms, face. My memory was shot with inexplicable holes, like forgetting which exit to take off the interstate. My heart sped up, flip-flopped in my chest. Itches I could never reach. Oil raw on the desert shoreline. Oil thick in the desert air from the ignition of hundreds of wells. Over and over again I see that helicopter dropping to the ground in slow motion. Always I am powerless to put out the flames.

There was a tightness in my chest, a tingling in my arms. One night when my face turned ashen, Tillie rushed me to the emergency room at Denver Hospital. "Inflammation," the doctor said, prescribing aspirin. I started having one beer about ten a.m. Another beer with my bologna and cheese sandwich. I stopped in at Pasquale's Bar for a pack of cigarettes and was the last to leave when they locked up at two a.m. I came home and vomited in the toilet. The next morning Tillie handed me my glasses.

"I think you lost these," was all she said. "This isn't doing your health any good. What are you thinking?"

"I vomited because of the headaches, not because of booze," I protested.

When I got replaced on the construction crew, the union couldn't protect me. My year at war was rewarded with downsizing and union-breaking and outsourcing. I kept searching for the enemy, someone to blame for my poverty, but the enemy shapeshifted from the person on the other end of the phone every time I called the Army to check on my disability claim, to the clerk in the post office, to ruffians hanging out on the street corner, to goose-stepping thugs massing on imaginary borders.

In order to be considered for permanent disability, I have to see the VA psychologist. I join the circle of men fidgeting in their chairs as we wait, men who have been forced to take up shelter in the shabby borderland between health and disease, a no-man's land, this quiet epidemic of homelessness.

"I keep telling them about all the gases I was exposed to over there," I say, "but the latest doctor tells me that no tests exist to show whether or not I was exposed to them. I get so tired of hearing that all medicine can do is treat symptoms. Within six months I slipped from being unemployed to unemployable. Today they tell me they've lost my disability claim. I need to fill it out again. I lost my apartment, my TV, my truck. Even with all my twitches and tremors, the doctors keep saying they can't pinpoint a cause."

"Are you depressed?" the VA psychologist asks.

"Yes. Because I'm sick." Seized by a force beyond my control, a firing of synapses makes my face a fish dance with eyes popping to the sides of my head, an internal war manifested in my face.

"Can't you live with your family?" the leader asks.

"My mom split after Dad got back from Nam. She died of leukemia while I was gone. My father was electrocuted on the construction site about a year after I got back from Desert Storm. A freak accident I couldn't get my mind around. I had to identify his body, collect his watch and wallet, make arrangements for burial. I gave the undertaker his string tie engraved with a horse's head, his money clip, his pocket knife, a picture of me in my Army uniform, his business card, Tyler Construction. Put these things in his casket, I said."

"Have you allowed yourself to grieve your father's death?" the leader asks.

"My dad got up, went to work, came home, ate meat and potatoes, went to bed and did it all over again, year after year. Then he died and all he had to show for it was a Chrysler that was hardly worth four hundred dollars. My girlfriend and I would be tooling along in Dad's car and something would trigger a memory, a song on the radio or a man walking with a swagger.

Tillie finally had enough and left. A week after the funeral, I was sitting in the attic of the house my father had rented. There were boxes with curled black-and-white photos of me riding my bike, key chains, checkbooks, coins, coupons never redeemed. At the bottom of the box was a letter that my father never sent me."

"Before you leave, I'll help you fill out your disability claim again," the doctor says as he rises, a signal that the session is over.

My head rolls on my neck. I wince, have to force out breaths as if I were a diver working from great depths. Right arm crosses over and grasps left shoulder. Bone and muscle and skin, that ultimate shelter from weather and blows, is holding me hostage, my body language a shout to be heard.

Cruising the mall, I hang out at the fountain looking for someone I can bum a smoke from. I feel a heavy hand on my shoulder. The brown hand is connected to a security guard.

"What the hell are you doing here again? I told you to keep your sorry ass out of here."

"Hey, this is America. Remember? Land of the free. Home of the brave."

"Don't give me no shit. You listening? Now go on before I toss you out with the garbage." He spins me around with his hand. I rise when the sun goes down. Sometimes I steal for a living. When I have the energy, I pick through dumpsters in search of something to eat or sell.

Scruffy hair, missing teeth, bad eyes, limp. I survive by trading everything not nailed down: tools, cans, even my blood until they tell me it's no longer safe.

The list of what God needs to take care of gets longer. The list of what I have control over gets shorter. Nights that there's no room in the shelter, I sleep under the freeway, in hallways, with an occasional sojourn in jail. On cold nights when I'm too late for even a cardboard box over my favorite grate, I find shelter from the wind by sleeping beneath the arms of Jesus on the bronze doors of St. Michael's cathedral. Unless the owner of the grocery store across the street comes over and chases me away.

"You scare off my customers," he says. The sound of trucks puts me to sleep. Some nights even makeshift space under the bridge is scarce. To settle myself down, I dream of Dad's house, with its heated, safe, well-lit rooms, doors with locks, electric switches that went on and off, stove that cooked nutritious meals. My deepest wound is no longer believing that I deserve a home. Dreams bleached away, I offend merely by existing.

Rush hour. Cabs speed down Fifth Street. Winter on the street. Homeless line up as if for interrogation. Having a bed for a night means guards and food lines, requires a watch-your-back, watch-your-mouth mentality. A world of down-on-our-luck people and pat-down searches at the door and grave lectures on the prohibition of bringing contraband into the shelter, this halfway house between the worlds of everything and nothing.

The front door of the Salvation Army Shelter is locked. "Open at 5," the sign says. "No one permitted to enter before that time." I take my place in line, with my yellowing white shirt and polyester pants that has a permanent wallet mark on the backside, all held together with an imitation leather belt. Scuffed oxfords. Stained threadbare raincoat left over from my military days. Grime of many miles on the road and wrinkles cover my face. Wild explosion of brown hair. Eyes a well of sadness.

My biggest problem at the moment is finding a wall to piss on without getting caught. In the midst of honking horns and squealing tires, I zigzag like a maniac across the busy street. Time inches along. Cool air becomes cold. The line of people waiting for dinner goes back two hundred feet. "This is the Sheraton of shelters," the man behind me says with all the arrogance of a head waiter at a pricey hotel. Resignation and the smell of unwashed clothes is in the air. A man and woman struggle to keep their small son in tow.

"The door is opening," someone at the head of the line shouts as everyone queues up for warmth and food. I'm the last one to receive the piece of paper that assures me that tonight I'll have a bed. But first there's a sermon before there'll be any eating. I file in and smell pot roast and musty hymnals and aging oak pews and disinfectant. I'm issued soap, a towel, a delousing agent.

"Strip and shower," the man in charge orders. I emerge from the warm water feeling human again. Ticket in hand, I walk upstairs where I'm issued underwear, a blue shirt, navy- blue slacks, socks and a pair of second-hand brown loafers, minus the pennies. Assigned bed number twelve.

I enter the jammed sanctuary and find a seat. The preacher drones on about sinners and saints, Jesus and the Devil, heaven and hell. My empty stomach is hell. That voice is my teacher telling me in high school to try harder, my commanding officer in the Gulf telling me to dig my foxhole deeper, my father telling me the board needs to be cut again because it won't fit the house he's building. People in the shelter look at me and then quickly glance away because, even in this place, my nervous hands and contorted face stand out.

"Sinners all, you are on the street because you've disobeyed God's law. Rejected Jesus' love," the preacher shouts. The next minute he oozes a fervent sweetness. "God is love." He's building up steam. Gesturing with his tattered Bible in one hand and shaking a clenched fist in the other, sweat rolls down the preacher's face, soaks his shirt collar through. Finally, the last amen, the benediction. *Now we'll eat*, I think, but the staff eats first, next the overnighters, then us transients.

A man with long white hair and beard shuffles up to me. "You're Harry's boy, aren't you?"

"Do I know you?" I stutter in surprise.

"I served with your father in Vietnam," the old man says. "I was sorry to hear about his passing."

Hanging onto the railing for balance, I descend the narrow stairway into the basement. Gradually my eyes adjust to the dim light, focus on the cinder-block walls and the cot with one brown blanket. Without knowing when it happened, I've crossed over to the shadow side.

Remove coat and shoes. Stow them under my pillow so no one can steal them. I pull my most prized possessions out of my knapsack: a creased paper and a framed picture.

"Dear Son,

I was glad to get your letter saying you were settling into life in the Persian Gulf. You ask why I never talked about my time in Viet Nam. That question has kept me up nights. I didn't know how to talk to you about that war with no landings, no front lines, no ultimate objectives.

Before I got to Vietnam all I knew was that tiny country was having communism shoved down its throat and we were there to give the people a chance to make their own choices.

I served with the Infantry unit Delta Company, 1st Battalion of the 502 Infantry, 101st Airborne Division. The reality was rising before dawn, having spent the night in a hole in the ground with only a tarp to keep out the rain. An uneasy silence before helicopters descended like angry hornets. Battlefield scenes that no John Wayne movie ever prepared me for. Viet Nam huts were destroyed with Zippo lighters. Old women slumped over rice bowls. Flies swarmed over bayoneted carcasses of water buffalo, chickens, pigs. Men and women and children were shot in the back as they ran. My company was considered the best in the battalion, but the barracks looked more like a fraternity than a military facility. No duty roster was posted. No one seemed responsible for anything. Our commanding officer hovered high above the battle, making notes on his clipboard.

When I came home, all I wanted was a good job, a

home, and family. Then your mother left and then died so suddenly. There was another war at home. I couldn't put my hands on the enemy here either. Now VA is telling me that my buddies are killing themselves faster than Charlie could. Guys who fought tooth and nail to stay alive. Guys who would have sold their mothers to get out of Nam in one piece. They're saying we're coming home and standing in line to blow our brains out? What a crock. We were suckers made to risk our lives in the wrong war, in the wrong place, at the wrong time. I don't believe that I deserve my Purple Heart.

What I want to tell you, Son, is being a man is following your own conscience no matter what anyone says. Doing what you care about. Being who you say you are. I wish I could have found the words to tell you before you had to find out what war was like for yourself. To tell you how proud of you I am.

Love, Dad"

In the picture my father stands on a ladder, hammer in hand, huge grin, his mouth moving with the beard, blue eyes burning like a pilot light. All it takes is a whiff of pine needles or the sound of a house going up, or the smell of scrambled eggs laced with tabasco sauce and a strong memory returns: I am six and Dad calls me from the top of the stairs. He's just stepped out of the shower and asks me to bring him a towel. My father is a naked giant. Losing my father is like living in a house with a picture window looking out over a forest, but then one day when I look out the window, the tallest pine has vanished, my shelter gone. Just before dozing off, I think I'm a child again, at home with the sound of winter rain on the roof, warmth rising from radiators, the smell of wet wool steaming.

THINK BEAUTY

Alice is out just as the sun comes up, shooting frame after frame of Indian paintbrush in every shade from yellow to orange to deepest magenta. Through her camera lens, the walls of the garden form a soft cradle of red and brown and green. Purple fireweed. White, pink, and multi-colored columbine. Lavender bluebells. And beyond the flowers, she photographs the mountains as they turn pink then violet. She aims her eye and becomes the golden eagle overhead, as it makes its lazy circles. Sitting down to reload film, Alice hears a car drive up the gravel drive. Caroline, Alice's best friend since childhood, is here to take her to the gym.

They drive down from the foothills, leave behind the perfume of apples, the tang of dying leaves, the country lane with its overarching trees that shade Alice's house all summer. Behind Caroline's curtain of blonde hair and large spectacles lurks a woman who changes personality behind the wheel. Riding with Caroline is a journey into the twilight zone of "what-ifs." Suddenly everyone in front of and behind her car becomes an ignoramus. She has her own unique theory about how to avoid traffic.

"If we leave now, it'll be rush hour and it'll take an hour to get to the gym. But if we leave in a half-hour, there'll be no traffic and it'll only take fifteen minutes to get there," Caroline says.

"Gee, we could actually pass ourselves," Alice says. They are on the freeway where grassy hills are terraced with condominiums. Orchards have been torn down to make room for identical houses. Meadows bloom with office buildings.

"Look at that fool trying to squeeze in on me. I see you! You're not going anywhere...." Her sentence dangles. Her neck is getting red with an anger so fierce that it makes Alice shudder at how fast it comes out of nowhere, her friend's face suddenly hard. For some, aging simply softens, mellows, ripens. For some, age turns them to stone.

"Calm down. Let the fire truck go by," Alice says.

"Fire my foot! There's *really* a fire before breakfast, right? Go ahead you ignoramus."

Asshole would have been Alice's profanity of choice.

"Caroline, you're right on that guy's bumper. Pull back a little."

"How old do you think I look?" Caroline asks. "You can tell me." Alice is used to Caroline's *non-sequiturs*, but this is a drastic U-turn even for Caroline.

"How old do you feel?" Alice asks diplomatically, as she pushes a corkscrew of red hair streaked with grey behind her ear. Her hips and bust are voluptuous rather than merely ample.

"Oh, twenty-six on my good days and sixty-four on my bad days, but my subconscious eye refuses to log anything past thirty-five. I'm thinking about getting a facelift," Caroline says. She is built like her mother: hollow bird bones and no flesh to spare. Her mouth turns down at the edges into a scowl.

"Do you really want to capitulate to a system that victimizes women by convincing them that being young and beautiful is what really counts?" Alice asks. "Why do you want to risk death? It could be a side effect of this surgery, you know."

"I want to make a pre-emptive strike now before I'm too old to enjoy the results."

"Couldn't you get a diamond stud in your belly button instead?" Alice sighs, realizing full well that Caroline is the kind of woman who knows every psychic within a ten-mile radius and once hired a color analyst who warned her never to wear bright yellow or liquid green. No earth colors. No ooze of apricot. No crush of dark raspberry. *Nothing too strong or definite. You are a summer. Semi-precious. Amethyst. Aquamarine. Colors of the sky.*

"So I'm shallow," Caroline says. "Shoot me."

Barker Gymnasium is filled with women pedaling like hell on their one-way trip to nowhere. Caroline wears leotards and a headband. She climbs on and hardly ever hits her stationary seat, manic, like a surfer catching waves, then crashing. She's up, she's down, sweating like crazy. Alice, in sweatpants and a red t-shirt, joins the group, fascinated by how much energy it takes to pursue beautiful thighs. In this room there is a great unveiling of the female body. Legs and underarms free of hair. Svelte torsos. Firm breasts. Alice treats her body the same way she treats her ivy and schefflera, with benign neglect. Living with a chef who elevates cooking to art is hard on her waistline. Sam, the master of Cordon Bleu and teriyaki steak with mushrooms and garlic mashed potatoes whipped to perfection. Twenty minutes later, Alice feels faint. Already her calves are beyond quivering.

"Take a sip of water," Caroline tells her. Alice is way beyond water, but Alice stays the course.

"Will you go with me to see a cosmetic surgeon? Please?" Caroline asks. Alice sits there, looking at her friend's profile, a younger Candice Bergen, and already knows that she'll accompany her friend because when they were thirteen and attended dancing school, the dancing teacher had pulled Alice to the center of the room after all the other girls had been chosen. *Would someone please dance with Alice McCullough?* the teacher had asked. Chatter subsided. Motion ceased. Caroline had brought Flash over to dance with Alice, an act of friendship that she's never forgotten. Caroline has always been the friend coming in Alice's front door when everyone else was going out. The sister Alice never had, the one to whom Alice could say, *come now, I need you,* and Caroline came, no questions asked. The friend who could say to her, *Why are you acting this way? You are wrong. Let's talk.*

Beauty was an endless topic growing up. When they were six, Alice and Caroline raided their mothers' closets for lavender chiffon nightgowns and rhinestones and paraded down the stairs like queens at a coronation ceremony. At ten, the girls had twirled and skipped and worn tutus to school. At thirteen they pored over *Glamour* and *Vanity Fair*.

"Don't you just love her hair?" Caroline had asked.

"But you *know* that model had a team of people working on her to make her look that good. Hours with a makeup artist. Soft-focus lighting," Alice had insisted, always the realist.

Alice waited and watched and exercised her chest while Caroline got her training bra, her period, feathered Farrah Fawcett hair, ears pierced, eyelashes curled. Alice waited while Caroline pushed five-five, five-six. Alice watched boys sniff around her best friend while her own face smoldered with acne. Iowa was on her chin and growing. While everyone else snuggled on hayrides, only Alice's head remained above blankets.

When she was thirteen, a girl in gym class had made fun of Alice's curly red hair. *Brillo pad, brillo pad*, she had taunted, and Alice knew she'd never be beautiful enough to be a model or a homecoming queen. *You don't look anything like Barbie. You don't fit in. You can't compete.* Within the security fence of chit-chat (*Do you like my hair better with bangs or without?*) and ads that preached that body hair was gross, the girls had shaved-bleached-dyed their way towards perfection. Weight. Breasts. Clothes. Alice and Caroline wore full skirts with petticoats that they soaked in sugar water and dried to make them stiff. Cinch belts. Tight skirt and sweater sets. They scrunched their feet into pointed-toe shoes. T-strap flats. Stiletto heels that poked holes in linoleum floors. They wore their hair in pageboys or pulled back in ponytails. Lipstick. Face powder. Blush. Mascara. Like tightrope walkers, they walked the line between appearing drab or cheap.

On long summer afternoons, they buttered each other in tanning oil and waited to see which boy would drop by.

Stretched out on a blanket in the backyard, Caroline looked like a Charlie's Angel in a blue bikini.

"Do you believe there's such a thing as true love?" Caroline had asked as they took turns reading *True Romance.* Lying beside her, Alice felt small, as if someday she might just disappear. The fact that her mother consoled her with, *You have inner beauty,* didn't help. She didn't want to be lit from within. Body image extended beyond weight, went deeper than tanned skin.

Alice's first camera was a Nikon with many attachments, the camera her eyes. Art was some candor. Some catharsis. Some mistakes. Some serendipity. She started shooting sunsets and waterfalls until one day she gathered all her pretty pictures of mountains and zinnias together and burned them. The day she awoke to the snarl of a chain saw rising above the sound of traffic, she grabbed her camera and ran to photograph the old silver maple in the front yard. For weeks, its shaggy bark had worn a large blue "X" that meant it was a Dead-Man-Walking. The city's crew had meted out a death sentence. A hazard tree. Alice aimed her camera up inside the hollow limbs and shot the rot-brown innards where limbs had been lost.

She stood in the darkroom watching the photographs develop out of nothing. *Why does this hollow tree move me? Is there truth here or merely beauty?*

Reluctantly Alice agrees to ride shotgun as Caroline tiptoes into the minefield of doctor appointments. "I'll go with you to see the cosmetic surgeon on one condition," Alice says.

"What's that?" Caroline asks.

"You let me photograph the whole process, from the doctor interviews, to the recovery room, to the day the bandages come off. I'll take care of you, too."

"That's blackmail."

"Not really. You know I'd take care of you anyway. But think of it as your contribution to my creative process."

"Okay, okay. You know you're the only one I trust to see me looking like a monster anyway." Two weeks later, Caroline and Alice are in a neighborhood ripe with exhaust fumes, where a woman could get an oil change and a facelift all on the same block if she wanted.

The doctor's office is on the top floor of a dark, glossy building just off Route 70. The waiting room has jungle wallpaper and large geode ashtrays next to fake plants. A table is littered with stacks of brochures advocating "easy breast augmentation." *Reader's Digest. Car and Driver. Cosmopolitan.* A woman across the room wears fishnet stockings and knee-high boots and looks like she's ignored her mother's warnings to stay out of the sun. Alice invents little movies in her mind: *That woman in black stiletto heels runs for the exit yelling Fire! Fire! Then trips as flames overtake her.*

"Fill out this questionnaire," the receptionist says as she snaps her gum. "Are you married, Caroline?"

"Are you?" Alice asks before Caroline can answer. Caroline gives her the 'shush' sign. "Go sit down," she hisses.

"What? Do they jack up the price if a person isn't married? How do you know this doctor isn't the kind who uses voodoo to remove double chins?"

"That's why I brought you along. The eternal skeptic."

A nurse beckons and Caroline follows her into the

exam room, secretly hoping that the doctor will chuckle at her foolishness and say *My dear, you are beautiful the way you are.* Alice lopes along behind, camera in hand.

"You may wait here," the nurse tells Alice.

"No, she's coming in with me," Caroline says, pulling her friend into the examination room. Dr. Sullivan looks like a young Willie Nelson: long ponytail, slight build, the same vintage string tie. He studies Caroline's face like an architect deciding where to insert a buttress. *Whir,* goes the light meter. The doctor turns and gives a toothy smile. *Flash,* goes the camera.

Caroline wears a forced grimace.

"Here. Take a look," the doctor says, handing Caroline a mirror. He's marked where he'll pull and cut in order to show her what to expect. How had she missed this landslide? "Your face is too narrow. You have no cheekbones," Dr. Sullivan says. And to think that Caroline had gone forty-two years without noticing. "You look worn out because of this," he says as he jiggles the loose pouch under her chin. "Of course, I can fix everything," he reassures her. "It wouldn't take a whole facelift. We could do facial contouring."

"What's that?"

"We liposuction fat from the stomach and inject it into your face. It would round out your face, erase those lines. Give you chic cheeks."

"What about the risks?" Caroline asks.

"People who do the best with cosmetic surgery are those with the right attitude. Those who think beauty. Take a lot of Vitamin C. And, of course, there are always the risks that can occur with any operation: infection, bleeding, and in rare instances, death. But let's not dwell on that."

"What does this surgery cost?"

"Five thousand dollars. Can I sign you up?"

"I'm going to get another opinion," Caroline says, trying to leave with a smidgen of self- esteem.

"The longer you wait, the worse it gets," this facial architect says, this master of persuasion. Caroline runs, shaken, for the door. Alice gathers her camera bag and follows.

Caroline maneuvers the car out of the parking lot.

"Here. I picked up this brochure for you," Alice says, handing over the paper. Clouds move in, a typical Colorado afternoon. "Dr. Sullivan holds seminars featuring a free drawing for a two-thousand-dollar gift certificate for cosmetic surgery. Guess who performs the surgery?"

"He had the nerve to charge me a hundred dollars to tell me I'm ugly," Caroline sighs.

"You're not ugly!" Alice shouts. "Why do you do this to yourself? Will this surgery make you happier, or stop you from getting old, or keep you from dying? I don't understand why you want to get a facelift. Talk to me."

"The new producer at the TV station came up to me after a show a couple of weeks ago and said, *'We should have done a better job with your makeup,'* the volume turned way up on her voice so that everyone in the studio heard. I was mortified. *'Unfortunately television empha- sizes what's already there and your eyes were lost in shadows.'* She didn't care that my newscast was all about the exposé of the cleanup at Rocky Flats. All she saw were these wrinkles stretching across my forehead," Caroline says as she pulls down the visor mirror, turns this way and that, pulling skin back with her fingers in an effort to regain a taut profile. "I've always had bags under my eyes, but now they've taken on whole new dimensions, with dark plains and fleshy mountains and overlapping ridges that create shadows over my cheekbones. What can it hurt to get a little nip here, tuck there?"

"But those bags are a dowry from your grandmother," Alice protests. "I love those bags."

"Last week when Jake and I ate at The Brown Palace, I saw him eyeing the young waitress. I caught my reflection in a mirror at the end of the room and didn't recognize myself. Suddenly, I can't read print closer than two feet away."

"Neither can I. But I chalk impaired vision up to God's way of taking sympathy on me. If I don't want to see how I look, all I have to do is take my glasses off," Alice says.

"Is there such a thing as a whole-body lift?" Caroline sighs. Doctor Number Two is in Cherry Creek. Dr. Lowell is a nationally known cosmetic surgeon. Caroline arrives in sunglasses and a black fedora without makeup, as his nurse had instructed, so that the doctor can get an unvarnished look. There is brown-velour furniture and oriental urns and a brass lamp that make Caroline and Alice feel as if they've wandered into someone's living room. Bookshelves hold real books rather than rummage-sale treasures displayed for decorative purposes. *Bonfire of the Vanities. Of Woman Born.*

Even early on a Saturday morning, the waiting room is mobbed. Wall-to-wall rhinoplasties. Two women lean in to discuss the peels and lipos they got last year and Alice wishes she could slide under the rug. From behind her *Newsweek,* she checks out the other women in their L. L.

Bean turtlenecks and duck boots, and fantasizes about their sex lives: *Do they leave the duck boots on? Do their lovers know they're sleeping with a new, improved model?*

"There's little pain involved. You'll be back to work in a few days," the nurse says into the phone casually, as if the invisible patient on the other end were scheduling a facial or a haircut. A nurse, with the bone structure and lustrous hair that movie stars covet, comes towards them, manicured hand extended. She's wearing a Donna Karan suit, the most stylish uniform that Alice has ever seen.

While Caroline is ushered into a room to watch a videotape, Alice leafs through copies of *Vogue* and the *Wall Street Journal* and sees articles about Dr. Lowell's work, complete with before-and-after pictures. *The photographer's lens has to be out of focus. His composition is off center.*

Caroline is prepared to hate Dr. Lowell, but he's warm and charming, more like a priest to whom she can confess her sins and secret longings. He is very tall, with white hair and an aquiline nose. He strides across the room, the epitome of *bonhomie. Joie de vivre.* Late fifties, maybe early sixties. He sits behind his mahogany desk as Caroline balances on the edge of a wooden chair. Alice hovers near a wall, camera in hand.

"How old are you, Caroline?"

"Forty-two."

"Are you married?"

"No."

"How long have you been thinking about getting a facelift?"

"On and off for a couple of years."

"What do you hope that a facelift will do for you?"

"I don't know quite how to answer that. Just to improve my confidence, I guess. I'm a TV newscaster for the local station. I want to take some action before they tell me I have to do something."

Dr. Lowell makes her stand as he explores her face with unforgiving eyes. It is worse than Caroline had feared. "First we have to take the bulb off the end of your nose," he says, leaving Caroline slack-jawed with shock. He's pointing at her Lowderback nose, a flat-topped, ski-jump affair. She has never considered her nose a defect to be corrected. *Who would I be without my grandmother's nose?* Alice finishes one roll of film and loads a new one.

Dr. Lowell seems more compassionate than the other doctor, or maybe it's only that Caroline's vanity is so badly damaged that nothing he says comes as a surprise. Yes, Caroline's face is narrow, her skin sags. But he seems to understand her sentimental attachment to her nose. He doesn't mention "chic cheeks." He seems to possess more wisdom than he needs to verbalize. He addresses Caroline as a whole person instead of seeing only the sag in her jowl. For only ten-thousand dollars, he can give her an improved version of her old face that her family and friends can still recognize.

The nurse leads Caroline and Alice to a sunroom with a spectacular view of a Japanese garden, where bonsai trees have been pruned into perfect domes. As they sit down at an oriental table, the nurse hands Caroline a paper upon which the doctor has written the procedures he recommends. There is a bewildering array of credentials and names of organizations to which Dr. Lowell belongs. "Be sure he's board-certified," Alice had warned her.

But certified by whom? And what's the difference between "Board Certified in Plastic Surgery" and "Board Certified Plastic Surgeon?" How much experience is enough?

"If you want a particular date, it would be best if you scheduled today. We'll need a deposit of one-thousand-three-hundred-fifty dollars now," the nurse says. "The balance must be received three weeks before the scheduled operation date." Good-sport smile pasted on her face, tense shoulders hunched up to her ears, Caroline decides to go for the stripped-down model and just have the bags removed from under her eyes. A little tuck in the forehead.

Caroline hurries out of the office with Alice loping behind.

"Just give me a paper bag to pull over my face," Caroline moans as she maneuvers the car out of the parking lot. The street is empty, the storefronts dark. Old sycamores line the boulevard, their limbs overhead making a dark tunnel with streetlights caught in the fog.

"So November tenth is the day. How much is this going to set you back?" Alice asks.

"The price of a used car. I could shop around for a lower fee, but do I really want to trust my face to a bargain-basement surgeon?"

"Good point. Radical change, the kind that would give you a leg up, has always been your favorite fantasy," Alice says. "And I suppose physical changes *should* be the easiest. But you know, no one in polite society will ever say, *Gee Caroline, you look great—you've had your eyes lifted, neck improved, lips jet-puffed. How becoming.*"

"But they certainly will notice that something's

different."

"Why don't you just let me take you out for a drink and tell you, *You look so beautiful today and I know it's your soul shining through*? I'll just keep saying it until you believe it. Have you told Jake you're planning to have surgery?"

"Not yet. Soon," Caroline says. "I wish I were more like you. You don't seem to care what people think."

"I learned a long time ago, back when my photographs were still being rejected and when I got passed over for grants, that if I didn't believe in my work, no one else would either. That's about the same time that I gave up wearing high heels and wonderbras and lip liner. Now I wear cowboy boots and no one has ever complained."

"If I try to claim my own space, Jake says I'm aggressive. Pushy. But if he does it, he's being assertive."

"It's not aggressive to tell him what you need," Alice says.

The day of surgery, Alice and Caroline arrive at the hospital and wait in a room that could easily be a bus station. They walk up the corridor, past windows that throw rays on framed portraits of Board members as if they were portraits of saints in a cathedral. There is the admitting desk, the "visitor's section" with its cheap hard-backed chairs, painted bright orange for optimism. Even this early in the morning, the TV is beaming news that no one is listening to, the on-off button suspended high out of reach. Across the room, a man holds a woman's hand while she softly cries.

"It's hell being awake at 5:30 a.m. You're lucky that we're joined at the hip," Alice grumbles. Caroline's name is called. "Break a leg," Alice says, "or whatever."

"This is no play," Caroline says as she rises to leave.

"Could have fooled me," Alice says. "I'll be here when you wake up."

Then Caroline is gone, follows her escort to the locker room where she takes off her clothes and puts on a paper surgery gown. In a hushed tone, the nurse leads Caroline to the small examining room. The knot in her stomach becomes a stone.

"How are you?"

"Terribly nervous."

"We'll give you some Valium to relax you." Then Caroline is rolling down narrow halls on a gurney, stripped of clothes and personality and identity, suspended in a state that is neither grace nor damnation. Flesh waiting on a table for the sculptor's chisel. Dr. Lowell squeezes her hand paternally. "It's time now," the nurse says. The room bleaches to white, then nothing.

The room is dark and Caroline hears someone say, "How are you feeling?" It is Alice's voice. A familiar hand squeezes Caroline's, but she can't see anything because there are wet compresses on her eyes. The head of the bed and her knees are elevated. She's waking up in a different room than she went to sleep. Everything in the vicinity of her head is tender and she knows better than to try to move. Swimming back into consciousness takes longer than it should. She wants to drift out to sea again. Her face is the size of a pumpkin and growing.

"How long was I under?"

"Almost three hours."

"The bandages are too tight," Caroline whispers. It

feels like a strap has been cinched under her chin and over the top of her head. Bandages encircle her head and neck leaving only her face uncovered, except for the compresses on her eyes. Everyone has told her that there would be little pain associated with this surgery. They lied. But the pain is nothing compared to the roiling of her stomach.

"The bandages are loose," Alice says softly.

"No. No. They're too tight," Caroline pleads. Alice squeezes her hand and slowly it dawns on Caroline that it is not the bandages, but her face that is tight. *Good God, what have I done?* Alice leaves and Caroline dozes back to sleep. Every couple of hours she's awakened by a nurse changing the compresses. Around midnight, the pain sharpens. A severe headache develops.

"May I please have something for pain?" she asks the nurse.

"Not time yet. Another forty-five minutes."

Time passes. Caroline asks again. This time the nurse relents. She must use the bathroom, so the nurse removes the compresses and helps her swing her legs over the edge of the bed. Nausea rolls in. Only able to open her swollen eyes a crack, Caroline stands at the sink and tilts her head back so that she can see herself in the mirror.

"Don't look," the nurse says, "please don't look." Her voice is soft, her concern evident. Caroline catches a quick look and realizes she's just landed in a Brueghel painting. She lowers her head and the nurse helps her back to bed.

Overnight the world has turned white; three inches of snow paint tree bark and brown soil into silhouettes of light and dark. The high mountain angels have been busy making powder, laying a tracery, a light mantilla over every surface. Crouched within her oversized scarf, Caroline prepares to go home. There is a long list of instructions: *Don't wash your hair for a week. Keep your head movements to a minimum. No heavy lifting. No leaning over.*

Alice drives Caroline back to her home in the foothills, leads her to her own four-poster bed. A silvery mist slowly rises off the meadow. Far off there is a cry of wild geese. Alice puts new compresses on Caroline's eyes and goes to the kitchen to make lunch. Caroline's scalp is tender to the touch—not hers exactly, a foreign object. Other parts are numb. She feels the swelling and the heavy metal staples from the forehead incision that pulls together two folds of skin.

"Here's your lunch," Alice says as she sets the tray of tomato soup on the bedside table and starts to feed Caroline.

"This feels like when I was a little girl and was sick," Caroline says. "I lay in our quiet house and had my mother's attention all to myself. She'd make a fuss and puff up the pillows, bring juice and water always with the curved glass straw. She'd read me *Grimm's Fairy Tales.*"

"In those stories, a passive woman was good, a catatonic one even better," Alice says. "There was no reason to stun a prince with intelligence, or kindness, or business sense, or wit. All that was required was the right shade of blush. The thickness of mascara. Back then beauty was simpler. A good daughter didn't get piercings or tattoos. A good daughter did what she was told. Eternally attractive, but demure. We were told that if we kept our legs locked, everything would be all right."

"Mama would sit at the corner table and make her

grocery list and I was in her marginal vision, her love indirect, like that glass straw," Caroline says.

"I can still see your mother decked out in her pumps and gloves and cameo brooches. Remember how we used to cruise main street in your parent's car listening to Elvis, and bought bags full of hot doughnuts from Dunkin' Donuts? How I wanted Peter to ask me to the homecoming dance the year we were juniors, and how hurt I was when he asked you instead?"

"I watched while you threw your own private girl-revolution at the tyranny of thinness and pert noses," Caroline says. "Wasn't that about the same time that you became a serious photographer?"

"My sale of pictures of that old maple to *National Geographic* was the turning point. But don't forget all those dead-end jobs that fed my photography habit. My stint as a teacher's assistant reading *Henny-Penny* to twenty-eight four-year-olds. Selling Electrolux sweepers door-to-door. Reshelving books at the library."

"Those were hard years for me too," Caroline says. "Selling ads for the TV station. Three years as 'Weather Girl.'"

"Why did we grow up thinking that we had to shrink our souls down to petite size? Why not embrace earthy goddess figures? Ample bosoms? Wide, giver-of-life hips? Why did we believe that we were forbidden to show anger or disagree with anyone? Why did we buy into all that emphasis on being 'nice?'" Alice carries the empty dishes to the table by the window.

"Well, I've at least gotten over that. But I'm still hooked on keeping up appearances. What are you going to do with all those photos you took of me?" Caroline asks.

"They'll be included in my exhibit at the gallery. I'm calling the series 'Think Beauty.' Women building houses, fishing in mountain streams, nursing babies, performing surgery. A woman with one breast. A woman putting on her prosthetic leg. Women with wrinkles and glass eyes."

"And your best friend swathed in bandages," Caroline says, taking a sip through the straw.

"And still beautiful."

"Help me to the john." Alice guides Caroline to the bathroom, waits for her friend by the door. Caroline pats her hands dry and sneaks the first look at her new face. Purple-blue bruises cover her eye sockets. Black stitches are visible along the inside crease of her lids all the way to the corners of her eyes. Gone are the familiar furrows between her eyebrows. Gone is the ability to move her forehead. Her mouth is pulled into a tight horizontal line. Her face is swollen, making her look like Alfred E. Newman of MAD Magazine fame. *Please, dear God, don't let me end up looking like a Kewpie doll.*

The bedroom window is open. Trees creak in a gust of wind. Cars accelerate up the hill.

Far off a siren wails. Something rattles in the bushes.

"Over there," Alice says, pointing at a large shape half-hidden in a clump of snow-covered Pfitzers. "See it?" There is a quick glimpse of sleek hindquarters as a deer slips through the shrubs and disappears into the gloom.

"Jake is having an affair," Caroline says as she rolls back into bed, carefully bracing her body, as if her head might break. "We made love for the last time and I didn't even know that we were saying good-bye. That's why I was so upset the other day. Sorry to take it out on you."

"Hey, it's that poor guy in the fire truck who I felt sorry

for," Alice says.

"I never thought I'd reach middle-age and not have a husband. I'm around people all day at the television station, but it's not the same as having a mate. Maybe I'm just unlovable. Is it fair to hold a few mistakes against Jake? He *could* change," Caroline says.

"This is true. But he has to *want* to change first. You try too hard. Love is like the butterfly I tried to photograph last summer. The more I chased it, the farther away it flew. But when I sat down to rest, it landed on a branch right in front of me."

"I thought if Jake were happy, then I'd be happy. Pleasing him. Keeping him. How did you know that Sam loved you?"

"We were on a train many years ago coming back from Pueblo," Alice says. "I was sitting by the window, Sam beside me, Colorado prairie flying past. There was a nosy toddler hanging over the back of her seat, looking at us as I told Sam that I wasn't ready to marry him and waited for him to explode or cry or plead his case," Alice says as she gives Caroline more soup, a sip of Chamomile tea. "But he only sat there, as if he'd expected my decision all along, as if my breaking up with him were a foregone conclusion. *I know I could never persuade you. It's your choice to stay or to leave,* was all he said. Two days later I was rushing back into his arms. A month later you were the Maid of Honor at our wedding. His simple phrase of acceptance, with its offer of freedom, chained me more completely to Sam than any wild declaration of love ever could have. He says he fell in love with my sense of humor."

"I could use a joke," Caroline says.

"Have you heard the joke about the woman who

confused her Valium with her birth control pills? She has fourteen kids, but she doesn't much care."

"Oh, oh, it hurts to laugh," Caroline says as she cradles her head in her hands. "My turn. What is the difference between how a man impresses a woman and how a woman impresses a man?"

"I give."

"A man impresses a woman by wining, dining, calling, hugging, holding, complimenting, giving jewelry, writing love letters. A woman impresses a man by showing up naked with a pack of beer." Laughter is the balm.

"Time for you to rest," Alice says as she renews Caroline's wet compresses, helps her brush her teeth, gives her the sedative that Dr. Lowell prescribed. In a few days the bandages will come off, but tonight there is no need to talk. Snowmelt and lengthening days take hold.

This is the silent season of waiting for ice to break in the creek, for hummingbirds to return to the feeder, a time to heal. What a beautiful thing silence can be between friends.

THIS MIDDLE KINGDOM

Logs in the cabin walls shake and bitter cold makes the roof crack. The pager squeals and Solomon reaches over to the bedside stand to turn it off. Abbie groans and rolls over and stuffs the down quilt over her head. Solomon is already running across the icy floor, pulling on jeans and a sweater as he reaches for the phone.

"What is it?"

"Two cross-country skiers are lost on Silver Creek Ridge. No one's heard from them in six hours," Ed says from the communication center in Piedmont.

"I'll be there in ten minutes."

Abbie rises and pulls on a sweater over her flannel nightgown and begins to unwrap the house, pulling blankets down from the windows, great soft things, blue avalanches falling into her arms. The windows of the cabin are covered with frost. The fire in the Ben Franklin stove is practically out. Abbie lights the lamp in the living room and carefully lays the pile of shavings, larger sticks. Flames flicker up from between grated teeth. *More, more,* the black toad hisses, always digesting, always dying down. Flames so hypnotic with their shushing sound, their chiding.

"You promised me that you'd not go every time your pager rings," Abbie says. Already Solomon is zipping up his parka. "I don't understand why you feel you have to put your life on the line for strangers. Your problem is that you think no one is as capable as you," Abbie says with a kiss.

"I'll be back before you even miss me," he says as she holds the cabin door open wide, letting in a burst of snow. Solomon has a drooping mustache and curly blonde hair that is now almost completely white. "Keeps my face warm when I'm skiing," he says when Abbie complains that her skin is chafed after they make love.

Solomon breathes in the sharp smell of pine needles, and heaves his winter parka, a fifty-pound lifesaving kit, into the trunk of the Subaru. Solomon drives down the curving road towards town, thankful for his four-wheel drive as he passes entombed cars and cabins up to their eyelids in snow. Piedmont is a sleepy silver-mining relic that is threatening to become the next Aspen. Hills rise on all sides so that any trail leading out of town must dip and cross, sidle and take chances. Rifts of the hills open into each other. There is one main street with no building taller than two stories. No traffic lights. One stop sign. People die here with shocking regularity because they take big risks rock climbing on steep cliffs or barreling down swift rivers or catapulting off icy slopes.

He parks the car in front of the communications cabin, a twelve-by-twelve-foot cubicle, the nerve center for

Rocky Mountain Rescue. "What do we have?" Solomon asks as he removes his gloves, rubs his hands together. The log walls are covered with topographical maps that are laminated and mounted on foam board. The base radio squawks, then is silent. Yellow legal pads covered with notes lie on the blue linoleum counter that runs the length of the far wall. Ed and Alan and Paul and John and Alex stand around. Winter shows on their faces.

Down vests make their shoulders huge. The mood is black.

"Two cross-country skiers are lost somewhere near Silver Creek Ridge. It's a known avalanche area. We don't know if they made it out or not," Ed says.

"Still no communication from them?"

"No."

"What do we know about these people?"

"Charles and Vanessa Hanson. An investment banker from Denver and his wife," John says. "They were warned that Silver Creek is an avalanche-prone valley, that it's dangerous because it climbs almost three-thousand vertical feet over five miles to an exposed saddle at the south end. But they wouldn't listen. 'I've got my cell phone with me,' Hanson said when he checked in at the trailhead. 'Snow is what we came for and avalanches, well, you can't do much about them.'"

"Nothing except avoid them. The cell phone won't do them any good if they're out of range or at the bottom of an avalanche. Weekend sportsmen who think they know everything about the high country are such a pain. And we're the ones who have to save their butts."

Solomon is the 501, the one in charge, and knows, whether good or bad, the outcome will be on his head.

That's why he keeps his pager on, his pack ready. He phones Charles Hanson's brother, Vanessa Hanson's sister, poking and prodding, hits them with hard questions: What kind of equipment do they have with them? How much experience have they had in the mountains? What kind of physical shape are they in? Do they take any medications? Have they been fighting lately? Are they out of work? Are they likely to become excited, easily disoriented? Will they sit down and die?

"Any luck finding a Jolly Green Giant?"

"No, but there is a Chinook helicopter who's willing to fly over the Continental Divide from Fort Carson. The weather being so bad and all, they're not sure they can make it from Colorado Springs, but they're willing to try," Paul says.

"What do you think the chances are for the skiers getting out?" Ed asks.

Solomon turns and holds out his right hand, and presses forefinger to thumb, making a zero. On the mountain, life can be fleeting and moments of true safety rare. Even experienced winter mountaineers can get turned around in conditions so bad they can hardly see. The first rule of the rescue team is to create no new victims. Protect yourself. Protect your teammates. Protect the victim. Piedmont Rescue is about experienced urgency, adrenaline, confusion, risk, cold water, rockfall, crisp air, and endless expanses of ice. When the temperature drops, the world becomes brilliant diamond chips. More than once Solomon has recovered a man's body frozen in an attitude of running, an expression of astonishment on his face.

Piedmont, Colorado. Population six hundred and fifty when all the aunts and uncles are home for the holidays. A one-stop-sign town where everybody knows who everybody else is sleeping with, who just got laid off, who's just lost his home to bankruptcy. After a divorce, Abbie had taken off with all her earthly belongings packed into the back of her truck and headed west out of Denver, up Route 70 into the Rockies to Piedmont, a town that prided itself on straight talk and its help-each-other spirit of survival. No fancy clothes, no trophy houses, no gold bangles on women's arms.

Twelve years ago, after a string of work-a-day-drone jobs as a stagehand and slinging garbage into big trucks, Solomon came to Piedmont to loaf along trout streams, to be lost for hours in autumn woods. Solomon lives for the feel of the wilderness, vast spaces threaded by railroads with forlorn stations, where houses stand alone and trucks crawl along back roads, and above everything looms the immovable, ancient mountains. Mt. Piedmont can be a good-natured somnolent giant or a ten-megaton Old Testament God that can humiliate a man, can force him to beg for mercy.

The autumn after Solomon moved to Piedmont, Abbie had driven by in her red pick-up truck and then he ran into her again in the post office. She was pretty in a rangy Katherine Hepburn, brassy voice kind of way. Abbie had no visible means of support and small-town tongues wagged about her love life: a divorce and then another broken relationship just before she moved to Piedmont. "She's hoping she'll meet husband number two on the Rescue Team," Carol, the post office clerk, told Solomon with a wink. "Look out for that one, Solomon. She wants to be rescued herself," Carol had laughed.

For the next six months, every time their paths crossed, Abbie and Solomon had bantered and sparred, sexual innuendo just below the surface. The attraction, the dancing around each other became a ritual that, for almost a year, wasn't acted upon. There's no such thing as anonymous sex in a town as small as Piedmont. Casual sex maybe, but it was never a secret for long.

At first, Solomon only allowed himself to think about Abbie a few minutes each night. And then he was aware how his body yearned, how endearing her eyes were, an exciting mix between green and brown. How she stuttered when she got excited. Dimples in both cheeks when she smiled. Lying alone in his bed, Solomon often heard coyotes as they spoke in sounds very much like the human voice, rising, falling, one coyote amorous, the other coy, and he understood when their dialogue ended in one last howl of longing.

The first time Solomon watched Abbie climb, a new kind of intimacy was formed as they moved in unison without a single word or touch. They learned when to speak and when not to, what to say to each other when they were frightened, how to praise each other when they succeeded. Danger was seductive. Solomon loved how Abbie's whole being was able to say *yes* as her intelligence and skill were transformed into strong, sure movement over snow or rock or ice.

Snow rises too deep to measure on either side of the path as it twists and turns through the Engelmann spruce. The mountain rescue team skims along the spine of Silver Creek Ridge, the last place the missing skiers were known to be, avalanche country. The wind-chill factor hovers close to zero. Snow in the foreground blends with snow in the background, forming one monochromatic image making it difficult to tell how close the rescue team is to hitting rocks.

Sno-Cats, with Solomon in the lead, cover the eight miles to the Piedmont Hut, a simple log building with eight bunks, a wood stove, and a small deck that looks west over a creek to an open bowl on the east side of the mountain. They unload their winter packs full of medical kits and freeze-dried food and emergency stove and fuel. Paul starts a fire. Len shovels off the roof. Alan, part of the team for six years, his blue eyes intent, huddles on a bench over his food, two days of thick brown beard drifting across the wide jaw that makes him a lady magnet. He cuts big bites off a huge chunk of cheese. He's known for eating vast quantities of food and still being a lean climbing machine.

"I'll never understand people who decide to cross-country ski in avalanche country," Ed says, blowing on his hands as he starts to set up the remote radio station. He has a large head of long red hair, a pronounced beak and the wiry body of a rock climber.

"Lowlanders can be so stupid," Alan says, wiping crumbs off his mouth.

"Cyril has all kinds of plans for how he's going to change our team, wants to make it a paid, all-professional crew," Len says. "With all these tourists moving in, pretty soon there isn't going to be any more wilderness. No place where a person can't reach a road in a day or two of walking. No place without satellites and cell phones."

"Let's get out there and find them." Solomon designates who will ride on which snowmobile. Two Sno-

Cats, four snowmobiles. It takes twenty minutes to get organized, then they roar out into an alien world as snow rises three and four feet deep on either side of the path, as it twists and turns through miles of Engelmann spruce and open meadows along the broad spine of Silver Creek Ridge. Snow falls steadily.

The team climbs so high that there are only krummholz, wind-sculpted, stunted trees which have been shaped into grotesque forms by ice crystals, whipped by erosive blasts of wind. Drifts six and eight feet deep are forming, with huge dry pockets blowing between them. Did they string out on the trek down the avalanche trap of Silver Creek, lose sight of each other, fall backward in the snow, lie exhausted in the powder? Did they make a wrong turn, have a map that was no longer valid? Were they able to make a snow cave that wouldn't collapse? Did they panic?

Abbie washes dishes and shovels off the porch and can't sit still. It isn't even nine yet. A day of worry stretches before her. She pulls on her sweater and jeans, runs a comb through her shoulder-length black hair, turns on the radio. The cabin is full of NPR, Bob Edwards' melodious bass: "Charles Hanson, prominent Denver financier and venture capitalist and his wife Vanessa are missing high in the Rockies. A rescue team is being launched but has been delayed because of blizzard conditions." She pulls on snow pants over her jeans, puts on her down jacket and gloves, and heads her truck towards town.

Long ago, Abbie had learned that it was easier for Solomon to climb a steep slope, to rescue a stranger than it was for him to sit with her in front of the fire discussing why his first marriage had failed, or how they were going to scrounge next month's mortgage payment. Her husband, the classic strong, silent westerner. She had learned to accept Solomon's coming- back-from-another-world demeanor every time he returned home after a rescue, that startled look when he suddenly remembered that he had a wife, a calendar, a list of obligations in the real world. It was only by a remark here and a fact let slip there that Abbie had pieced together Solomon's life before mountain living: his years in San Francisco as an anti-war activist seeking peace, love, and Rock 'n Roll. That a Volkswagen bus had been his first home until a room in a commune opened up.

Abbie mans the radio in the communications cabin. Cyril, the Deputy Sheriff, is legally in charge, but Solomon is the leader on the mountain. Cyril is the one who rants at meetings about insurance liability and personal injury lawyers and fund-raising benefits and budgets, but Solomon is the one struggling to bolster his team's waning morale.

"The rescue team won't even be able to see their ski tips in this kind of weather," Cyril says. "I think we should bomb the Silver Creek valley. That way we can shake down any avalanches that may threaten the road. Then I can send plows in." Everything about Cyril is oversize: his pug nose, the volume of his voice, his ample belly.

"Sounds mighty dangerous to me," Abbie says. "Avalanches aren't that simple. Bombing may not release all of them. I've found a helicopter that's willing to fly in bad weather," Abbie says as she sketches out on a laminated topographical map a probable route that the missing skiers might have taken.

"Sorry. I can't okay that," Cyril says as he flips through a huge three-ring resource binder. He stands up, filling the room. His blue eyes are rimmed in red.

"Why do you have to make everything a pissing contest?" Abbie snaps. "Solomon knows what he's doing. He's been at it longer than you've been Deputy."

The radio squeals and Abbie picks up the receiver. "Rescue team to base. Over."

"Piedmont here. Any sign of the skiers?" Abbie asks over the receiver. "Negative. What are you doing there?" Solomon asks.

"Making myself useful," Abbie says. Crackle. Silence.

"You're breaking up. I didn't copy that. Have you heard anything from the Hansons?" Solomon shouts.

"Negative," Abbie says. "Cyril wants to try bombing the avalanche area, wants to send more men and dogs."

"Tell Cyril no dogs, no bombing, no more people in the field that I'll have to keep track of. We don't need any avalanche triggers. The team is going out on skis. We're at the location the Hansons were last seen."

"Be careful," Abbie says, but Solomon is gone before she can say, "over and out."

Sno-Cats float over snow the way a boat floats in water. The machines squat on the open bench looking like moon-landing crafts from another planet: the sourceless light, the cold, the steady wind, the difficulty in hearing, the shortage of oxygen. Snow has stopped falling and the sun is out, blinding in its purity. Solomon stops his snowmobile at Taylor Pass and looks back at the base of the cornice with binoculars. There are avalanche debris piles and dark objects lying on the snow. Much of the valley is in dark timber. He begins with one clump of trees, Ed with another. Above the wind, the men shout and holler as they look for signs of digging, broken branches, anything to indicate that two people have camped here. They investigate sixteen tree clumps and find nothing, head up the ridge to the peak. It is blowing hard now, maybe fifty miles per hour, but Solomon takes his gloves off, unzips his parka because he's sweating, sucking wind in the thin air as he breaks a trail in the snow.

Through binoculars, Solomon sees the rubble and fracture lines of an avalanche, a boundary sharply defined by a crack. The activity looks recent, a good sign since it's unlikely that there would be another avalanche in the same area. But to be safe, they need to keep weight on the ice to a minimum. Solomon signals to the other rescuers that they should head back to the hut, that he and Ed will check out that last black shadow one hundred yards ahead on the trail. Switching to skis, Solomon and Ed top out on another snow cliff and stop to wipe fog off their goggles. Sun bounces off diamond snow. Without saying a word, Ed and Solomon start avalanche busting, anticipating each other's moves like an intricate ballet as they approach the avalanche path as high as they can. Solomon takes his cut at the slide path while Ed watches from a secure position behind a tree. Then Solomon watches while Ed takes a cut, going farther down the slope. In leapfrog fashion they cover the slide path, both aware that their combined weight, plus the cutting action of their skis, could act as a trigger.

Solomon heads down the slope, his eyes on the suspicious black shadow when a wall of snow hits him square and he falls through until his skis hit the hard base of old snow underneath. The snow along the wall of the gully begins to curl back toward the main current, taking Solomon with it. He is knee-deep in boiling snow, then waist-deep, then neck-deep.

Through ankles and knees, he feels his skis drift onto the fall line, but he is still erect, still on top of them. "If you're caught in an avalanche, try to ski out of it," the rescue manual instructs. But with his skis trapped under six feet of snow, he isn't going to ski out of anything. No time to cry out, no chance to outrace the white death, Solomon is frozen in his tracks.

Back in Piedmont, satellite trucks line up, their television lights bathing the communications cabin in a green glow. The small room is a blur of reporters and family members of Charles and Vanessa Hanson. The Deputy Sheriff is giving an interview. Someone offers Abbie a glass of beer, but she declines and gets on the radio to let the rescue team know that the cross-country skiers are safe.

"Home Base calling. Do you copy?" "Piedmont Hut here. Len speaking."

"Where's Solomon?"

"He and Ed are still out in the field."

"Tell him the Hansons are here in Piedmont." "Are they okay?"

"Affirmative."

"Great. We'll head back down as soon as Solomon and Ed come," Len says. "See you soon. Over and out," Abbie says.

High on youth and adrenaline and Coors, everyone is smiling, ebullient, the room exploding with noise. Vanessa

Hanson waves her bandaged hands for the camera, her blue and yellow Gore-Tex outfit shimmering under the camera lights. Charles Hanson poses, holding out a donation check to Cyril, both men grinning for the audience.

"Were you warned about avalanche danger?" one of the reporters from the *Denver Post* asks. "The sheriff says you were skiing out of bounds."

"We came for the snow," Charles Hanson insists.

"So, the snowstorm was what you wanted?"

"Silver Creek Pass is always a crapshoot anyway. We ended up one hundred eighty degrees off course and skied twenty miles south to Taylor Reservoir. We broke into a cabin to dry out and sleep. The next day we skied to the tiny store at the reservoir. From there we called the sheriff," Charles Hanson says.

"Are either of you injured?"

"I'm in good shape. My wife has frostbite on several fingers."

Abbie hears this man and woman proudly telling their tale of mountain survival and feels as if she's been slapped. The Hansons have no idea of the exhaustion and fear and cold Solomon and the other rescuers are going through on their behalf. Of all the acts of self-sacrifice and generosity the team members perform week in, week out. "Lost Skiers Come Out Alive," will be the headline in tomorrow's *Denver Post*. Abbie sits, arms folded across her chest, and watches the Deputy Sheriff tell about the dangers of mountain rescue while her husband is still high up in the mountains.

It's almost a relief to be weightless—an invisible force

sucks Solomon downward into the bluish-white snow as if neon light were shining from underneath. Falling like an angel into the snow's soft, welcoming arms, he closes his eyes and begs the mountain to spare his life.

Something in his brain explodes and suddenly Solomon makes two forward somersaults, like a pair of pants in a dryer. At the end of each revolution, the avalanche smashes him hard against the base, as if the mountain god were swinging a pack of ice against a rock to break it into smaller pieces. There's no pain, just a jolt that wrenches a grunt out of him each time ice hits. The avalanche removes his skis.

He struggles a little longer but realizes that it makes no sense to try to conquer ice and, at some point, stops. His passage from life seems less a tragedy than an acceptable, warm fact. Already he's dreaming, his mouth faintly blue, eyes closed, no longer fighting it when suddenly he's on the surface again in sunlight with Ed standing over him, reaching out his hand. Solomon spits a wad of snow out of his mouth and takes a deep breath, lies there dazed, getting back his wind.

"Are you hurt?" Ed asks

"I don't think so. Bruised a little maybe."

"Let's get you back to Piedmont so the Doc can check you out." "What about the lost skiers?"

"Screw them. Let's get you back to Abbie."

Rescuers trickle in from the mountain and congregate at Rusty's Bar, giddy even without alcohol. Everyone needs a shower. The beer quickly goes to people's heads because they're so exhausted. Men and women lounge on chairs, boots off, feet up on chairs, air dense with steam and smoke as survival stories are exchanged, an informal debriefing, lives linked by the danger they've just experienced.

"The avalanche back in 1989, now that was a bad one," Cyril says, leaning into the bar. "That sucker swept through the valley, broke windows, burst the lock on doors, lifted roofs right off. I was in the post office when it hit. I scrambled to dig myself out. In less than an hour, twenty-two people were lost. As quickly as it began, the storm was over," Cyril says to the crowd standing around.

Abbie throws her parka over a chair and orders a pizza and a coke and claims a table by the window so that she can watch for Solomon. Snow has stopped falling. Stars are just beginning to come out.

"There's a call for you, Abbie," the bartender says, and she runs for the phone.

"Abbie, it's me," Solomon says.

"Where are you?"

"The hospital."

"What happened?"

"Avalanche. Ed pulled me out."

"Are you okay?" Abbie yells.

"Just bruised, I think. I'm waiting to be taken for X-rays."

"I'm coming there."

"No, stay there. Ed is here with me. We'll come to Rusty's as soon as I'm done here. I don't want you on the roads," Solomon says, his voice showing more emotion than usual. The bar is full of mountaineers so large and hairy that it is hard to tell where beards end and sweaters begin. People with red faces and swollen knuckles and full steins move from table to table, gossiping about each other's latest sex partners or who refuses to rock climb with whom, or snow conditions, playing pool, throwing darts. Abbie's eyes light up as Solomon shuffles in, Ed close behind.

"You guys do great work," Lucy says to Solomon as she hands him a menu. "Have a drink on the house. And one for you too, Abbie, because you have to sit home and worry about him."

"Give me two burgers. I haven't eaten all day," Solomon says. Abbie helps him to the chair at her table, her hands touching his cheek, his shoulder, his back, reassuring herself that he is really okay. Abbie rises and plants a big kiss on Ed. He blushes three shades of red.

"That's for saving my husband," Abbie says, turning him loose.

"It really wasn't me. The mountain decided to let him live. One of his skis was sticking straight up. Good thing," Ed whispers in Abbie's ear, then heads across the room to play darts with Len.

"I want one of those," Solomon says, and Abbie obliges with a long, lingering kiss.

"The whole time that you and the team were yelling out Charles and Vanessa Hanson's names on the mountain, they were huddled around a wood stove sipping hot buttered rum and talking to reporters," Abbie says as she makes room for Solomon at the table.

"I heard," Solomon says gently. Exhaustion is a splint holding him up. "So, where are they now?"

"They were airlifted back to Denver about an hour ago. The woman needs medical treatment for frostbite on two fingers."

"This isn't worth it anymore." Solomon leans over and

pulls a paper from his parka. He walks across the room to the bar and holds out the paper to Cyril.

"What's this?" Cyril asks.

"My resignation from Mountain Rescue," Solomon says. "I didn't sign up to manage incidents and fill out paperwork and be second-guessed about every decision I make."

Cyril glares from under his bushy eyebrows. "That's not funny," Cyril says, rolling his eyes.

"No one's laughing," Abbie says as she puts her arms around her husband. "The Hansons walked out of the mountains and my husband almost died."

"You guys who volunteer need to grow up and turn pro," Cyril says.

"I don't want to turn 'pro.' If my ski hadn't stood straight up after the avalanche knocked it off, Ed would never have found me. Someone was trying to tell me something and I'd be a fool not to listen," Solomon says. The food arrives. The combination of warmth and nourishment and free beer finally teases his muscles to relax.

When the weather allows, Solomon and Abbie lead low-landers up into the mountains they love with all its extreme hazards: toppling seracs, avalanches, crevasses, altitude, rockfall. "You work so hard to get up the mountain, then you work even harder to get back down. Why?" a tourist asks Solomon.

"Skiing is about flying," Solomon tells the tourist as he turns around and gives Abbie a big smile because he knows that she understands how it feels to be suspended in air, skiing nonstop top to bottom as a rhythm sets in, a flow state, a Zen-like calm.

Now, after eleven years of marriage, the intimacy of climbing has held up even under such severe tests as withstanding the smell as they strip down to fragrant underwear and wet socks, the poke in the ribs Solomon gives Abbie in her sleep, pushing her toward the wall of the tent as it drips with condensation, the rude way he steps over her in the middle of the night as he heads outside to relieve himself.

It is all worth it when they see an eagle-wing embossed on snow, or awaken to mountain goats rooting outside their tent, in this middle kingdom, this land suspended between earth and sky. When Solomon rock climbs and fastens his rope through his harness and puts all his weight on the rope, he depends upon Abbie to keep him from falling as he rappels across the crevasse. Love is a leap of faith that they will both land safely on the other side.

SHIFT

It is seven in the morning as Demetri Cox drives toward the hospital. *"Sometimes I feel like getting in the car and driving and disappearing,"* Cecelia had said as they sat in the kitchen. Already the day promises to be another hot one. Nothing mars the cloudless blue sky, not a hint of an afternoon storm gathering behind brown mountain peaks to the west. From the outside, the hospital isn't much to look at: a box plopped down in the middle of chimney stacks and a concrete canyon. For the next twenty-four hours, only the present exists.

His white coat flaps, stethoscope bounces as the doctor runs, its weight a comfort, like a rosary for a priest. His pockets are full of bandage scissors and pens and notes to himself: *Call Cecelia. Sign off charts from yesterday.* The intercom honks. Flashing lights from the ambulance bay wash walls in crimson. Paramedics burst through doors pushing gurneys, puffing with exertion, pirates of silence. Two police officers follow close behind.

There are lots of hands putting in tubes, cutting off clothes. "Talk to me. Don't give me an attitude. I'm not your enemy." Dr. Cox goes to work on the boy, Hispanic, sixteen years old, hemorrhaging. A bullet to the abdomen must have hit the aorta or liver. Vomiting blood.

"BP 104/60, pulse 70. Two lines in. Need O negative blood."

"His crit is twenty-seven," a nurse says, relaying the patient's Hematocrit.

"Get blood gases stat," Cox barks, but already it's too late. The doctor grabs the rib spreader, cracks his chest, a dire step only done when there is nothing to lose. The boy's heart floats in a pool of blood like a drowned kitten. The doctor's hands continue to work inside the chest. *Squeeze--release. Squeeze--release.* And then a quiver. A quiver. Molecules of sodium, potassium, and calcium silently shift across membrane boundaries, create an electrical charge that awakens tiny muscle fibers all over the heart beating against his open palm. The nurse places moist towels over the wound. "Call the OR. We're on the way. Hold the elevator." Two nurses and the doctor run alongside to the operating room. After the OR team takes over, the doctor sits on a bench beside the elevator for a moment to catch his breath. "Thank you," he says to no one in particular, still adrenalized. No one answers back. The boy survives. Demetri Cox has told his wife more than once: *We are in a war and no one cares.*

The fall Demetri was a second-year medical student, he met Cecelia in Starbucks.

"What will you have?" she asked.

"Latte," he said. She rubbed the back of her hand

across her eyes. A strand of pale-blonde hair fell out of her ponytail, down behind her ear into the hollow of her collarbone. Demetri wanted to brush it off her neck, tuck it back into the elastic band, let the pad of his thumb rest very lightly in the curve below the bone. That hollow curved like a spoon. Feel her skin on his tongue. He asked her out and she accepted and they floated along on a pheromone tide throughout their time at Columbia and Demetri's residency. Demetri would have gladly followed Cecelia into a burning building, no questions asked. Romance, that perfume, intoxicant of the emotions, catalyst for things to come. Cecelia stopped him in his tracks. The way she threw back her hair, her slim hands as she handed him his coffee, fingers lingering longer than necessary. She left him breathless and giddy and flushed with love, or lust, or both. Hand tentatively touching knee. Stopping halfway through a revolving door for a kiss.

Spontaneous shared laughter that lit up their eyes. Salacious grazing of bodies while washing dishes.

Cecelia liked dancing, jazz, merlot wine, peppery food, passionate kissing, and books. When they met, she was studying to become a librarian. "Cooking is my gift to you," she said and when Demetri got off work, she'd have spaghetti with clam sauce and merlot waiting. He'd tell her about the patient who came in with his penis caught in a bottle, and they'd laugh and she'd spend the next hour reading him Octavio Paz: *"The time of love is neither great nor small; it is the perception of all times, of all lives in a single instant."*

8:30 a.m. "Dr. Cox? Joe White on Ambulance Five. How do you copy?" "Loud and clear."

"We're *en route* to your location. Code Ten with a forty-two-year-old male stabbed twice.

One stab wound right anterior chest about seventh or eighth intercostal space, midline to the nipple. No crepitus felt. Breath sounds are good on the right side at this time. He's also got a superficial stab wound about mid-abdomen, just above the umbilicus. Belly soft, not tender. I put two lines in him. BP is 106 palp, rate about 110, no shortness of breath. ETA is three minutes."

"Is there a sucking chest wound?"

"No. Right now everything is closed up. Good breath sounds on the right." "All right. We're expecting you. South lawn clear."

"Number Ten clear." By the time the patient arrives, his lung has collapsed. Dr. Cox makes an incision and runs a tube into his side to relieve pressure. This day is picking up speed, thumping along with heart sounds and coughs and curses. Phones ring. Doctors and nurses call out orders. Machines hiss and buzz. Being an ER doctor is a constant flood of cuts and bruises, aches and pains. Dr. Cox has to believe he can save them. Good days. Bad days. Kids with funny things up their noses, coins in their esophagi. An artist loses his sight. A musician his hearing. Three months ago, Cox had worked hard to save a kid shot by a gang member, only to see him return last week and, this time, die.

New patient in Room Three. "Sixty-five-year-old man, five-year cardiac history. Was in the bathroom. Wife heard him go down. Down time about ten minutes."

"Any lidocaine or bretylium given? Oh, there he goes. Everybody clear. Zap him again." He slides into a chaotic rhythm. This time he's gone. Dr. Cox calls it. Machines are turned off.

"Can I have a name on this gentleman? I like to know I'm talking to the right family. What time did we call it? Nine twenty-three," Dr. Cox says.

The air in the room feels almost too heavy to breathe. The terrible marble absence of life. The wife enters the room. "Don't leave me. I love you. I can't live without you." She picks up her husband's fan-shaped hands, which are now only a bunch of little bones.

Six months after they met, Demetri and Cecelia drove to New Jersey to tell her folks about their engagement. On a whim, Demetri pulled off to the side of the freeway, grabbed Cecelia's hand and pulled her over a grassy embankment. They made love there, barely concealed, while semis roared by.

Cecelia was full of surprises, like the day Demetri was so worried about whether or not he'd gotten his internship and the phone rang. When he picked it up, he heard her singing their song—*At last my love has come along*—they reveled in romance of the impromptu variety. Lit candles encircling the tub. A Chet Baker tape that made them weak, *My Funny Valentine*.

Reading *Lady Chatterley's Lover* while stroking each other's bodies. No one in medical school could explain the slight movement in the heart, the catch in the breath, the shiver when Demetri thought about making love with Cecelia. White bodies in the light of dawn, breasts, eyes, the never-satisfied mouth.

10:25 a.m. Control is an illusion, like a shift of snow before the avalanche engulfs everyone in sight. A police officer comes through the doors with a toddler in his arms who has nothing on but a wet paper diaper. The little boy is a bag of bones. He has fallen out of a window and the police officer is in shock. He clutches the child, won't let go. The officer babbles as Dr. Cox pries his fingers off. The doctor places his stethoscope on the tiny chest, then puts it back in his pocket and turns toward the window. It's raining outside. The toddler is very dead.

A girl in the waiting room keeps opening and closing a knife. Dr. Cox calls the security guard to stand by. She is a regular, has stopped taking her pills, is seventeen. She's been known to hit her head against the wall, to make little cuts on her wrists. Dr. Cox rings the psychiatrist on call. At the nurses' station, he hears the triage nurse say, "Sir, I'm sorry but we don't pull teeth."

Sometimes when Demetri first wakes up, he thinks he's back in the anatomy lab. Even before he had ever held a stethoscope or a reflex hammer or a patient's hand, he had been led into a room of strong-smelling formaldehyde corpses. Something deliberate and important was happening before his eyes besides learning the structure of the human body. That barn of a room was the initiation that forever separated Demetri, a neophyte doctor, from everyone on the outside.

The first week in the dissecting room, Professor Blair asked him where the ulnar nerve was and Demetri could not find it. The professor pointed it out far from where Demetri was looking. *But it's in the wrong place*, he had protested.

You'll learn soon enough that, in anatomy, it's the normal that is uncommon, his professor had said. The first year of medical school he was scared to probe any deeper than a patient's chief complaint, his past medical history, his medication list. Demetri learned how to think in negatives when he took a medical history, or performed a physical exam: No this, no that instead of good this or good that. Patients were diagnostic riddles to be solved, the patient lying on the bed before him shifting into a nameless thing. *Look at this cardiac arrest or this COPD patient.*

Soon after they were married, Demetri took Cecelia to Simm's Landing, a restaurant perched on the edge of the mountain. Denver's lights sparkled far below. They were celebrating her new job at the Denver Library. Reference Librarian. Medium-rare steak with mushrooms and shallots, asparagus spears drenched in lemon butter, potatoes baked to perfection. Demetri sat there looking at his wife and realized that, instead of seeing her slim white skin, he saw a neck stem of muscles, veins, nerves he'd sliced and pinned and studied that day in anatomy lab. Demetri was hooked on split-second decisions and coffee highs. Being the one in charge of the paddles as he shocked fibrillating hearts back to life.

Listen to this, he'd say as he read her a paragraph from one of his medical journals about the latest time-management study. Cecelia pretended to listen, then hid behind her book. Demetri thought their marriage was rolling along just fine.

11:20 a.m. The waiting room looks like a bomb shelter: men, women, children slumped against each other sleeping, crying, staring straight ahead. Dr. Cox is caring for an eighteen-year-old overdose. His lips look like white stones, his eyeballs filmy, glazed. Like trapeze artists who know exactly where to reach for a partner's waiting grip, nurses and doctors link up at breakneck speed to halt onrushing death.

"Increase the rate of Levophed and Isuprel and see what happens."

"How fast?"

"One-twenty."

"Do we have a pulse with that? Do we have any without CPR?"

"No. He's gone again."

"Initiate CPR. Turn the pacer on while I put the catheter in." "Is he gone?"

"He's trying to breathe. Does he have a pressure?"

"Yeah. I can feel a pulse down here real well." The patient's eyes stare at their own opacity. Dr. Cox knows the medical team is winning when he sees those eyes shift from the next realm back to the ER ceiling.

Before Cecelia moved in, Demetri's apartment had the smell of kitty litter and wilted plants and packaged cinnamon rolls growing stale on the counter. It was a one-room efficiency, three flights up. Back in those days, Cecelia would step out of the shower and say *Demetri,* and he knew by her tone of voice that she wanted him as he stood naked at the sink, shaving. She'd place her wet hands around his neck as Demetri lifted her off her feet into his arms, tossed her into the middle of their disheveled bed. Nights were filled with silent, sweaty struggles interrupted with outbursts of wild laughter, shrieks, gasping breaths.

Cecelia believed in order, tranquility, her home as safe haven. She believed that the neat, tidy surfaces of objects warded off misery, despair. She was constantly vigilant, said she loved being a librarian because the Dewey Decimal System never changed. Books remained in their proper places until summoned. The only violence she'd ever seen in the library was the day a little boy got his finger caught in the door and fainted.

He loved the way her head turned towards his on the pillow. Moonlight illuminated her neck, arms, thighs, silly knobs of knees. How she'd laugh in the middle of rumpled sheets, her closed book flung to the foot of the bed. Demetri slipped an arm around her while she slept peacefully, like a child, feet touching beneath the quilt. The streetlight was a blossom on the wall. She breathed in, moved closer at the feel of his arm. The smell of lilacs from the bush outside the window. The musky smell of sheets.

But always there were ER voices crowding their tiny apartment: *Do you have someone who can drive you home? This is tetanus toxoid. The same size of needle we use on kids, so it shouldn't bother you much. One, two, three, it's in.* Demetri always knew he had to show up for his next shift.

2:10 p.m. Demetri Cox loses all sense of time, knocked out of time by emergency after emergency. "What hurts, Ed?" The man's nose is bloodied, his face hamburger-red, matted hair, sun-bleached, clotted into dreadlocks. He looks at the doctor through a drunken haze.

"My left leg."

"Your left leg always hurts," the doctor says. Ed is known as a frequent flyer.

"He's here for his nose," the paramedic says. Ed was picked up on Capitol Hill, knocked unconscious by someone wielding a skateboard. It's the fourth time his nose has been broken. Other times he comes in with lice, or in need of a shower.

"I'm not taking a shower," the man says, even though no one has suggested it. Ed has AIDS.

"May I look at your nose?" Dr. Cox asks in his best professional manner, speaking quietly, slowly.

"No!"

"We need to help you," Dr. Cox says as he starts to examine him. The nose is totally smooshed. Ed doesn't want to cooperate. "Don't move," Dr. Cox says as he tries to put an IV line in. Blood drips out of the catheter onto his gloved hand. Blood is placed in four tubes. Fluids are given intravenously. Ed flails on the gurney, responds like a man under attack.

"Chill out, man," Cox says. All any patient wants is to have his needs met, be shown respect. Some just take a little longer to respond. There are certain universal truths. This is one.

"I'm coming back looking for you," Ed says. Maybe it's all bravado brought on by life on the streets, or a night of crack. Or maybe he's serious. The more immediate risk are his gyrations, the very real possibility that Ed might knock a needle into the doctor's hand. "This hospital ain't shit." Ed flops around on the gurney.

"In the last six months, how many partners have you had?"

"Shiiit."

"Okay, on an average. How many tricks a week?"

"That's hard to say."

"In a day?"

"Seven or eight."

"Were any of these bisexual?"

"How the hell do I know. If it's a date, I use rubbers." Ed yawns, coming off a cocaine high. Black spandex hugs his thighs. "But I'm out of rubbers. Got any?"

The doctor brings a box and Ed grabs a handful, like a kid at Halloween who's offered one Hershey bar but grabs a handful when a back is turned. A little Valium through his tubing and finally Ed lies still. Dr. Cox has seen all kinds. The patient who shot peanut butter in his veins. The time police called to say they'd found a penis in front of city hall. *"Do you have anyone missing one?"* they had inquired. And there was the man who had stuck rings up into interesting places. Everyone has a story. *"Sir, are you always sweaty when you're sick? What do you take for medicine? Your heart? Do you know where you are?"*

Nothing can stop people from stocking their cars with vodka and driving ninety miles per hour down highways heading for a night of love-making and dangerous speed. The first lesson that Demetri Cox learned as a young doctor was that he was responsible for life. The second lesson was that he'd never learn all he was supposed to know, never be as effective as he should be. All of a sudden, death was a "bad outcome." A new admission was a "hit." When he was still a resident, he was working in ER and saw a baby snuggled in her pink cotton jumpsuit about nine o'clock one evening. The little girl had a magnificent profusion of black curls and a face that could have graced an ad for baby food. Demetri took the history from the anxious parents: "Well baby, born full-term, not eating well. Fever for two days."

"Any trouble sleeping? Does she wake up and cry as if

she's in pain?" he had asked.

"Oh no. She sleeps peacefully."

Demetri had diagnosed gastroenteritis and sent her home. The next morning the mother found her dead in her crib. Demetri was working graveyard and the Chief Resident came to their apartment, woke him up and told him in a deep, solemn voice. But, before he even opened his mouth, Demetri knew what was coming. He walked around with a ton of bricks around his heart. In his tired-bordering-on-exhausted mind, Demetri had felt the shiver that goes with the reminder that all children are vulnerable.

Nightmares started. Demetri was standing in a courtroom in front of God, and everyone was saying: "You screwed up. You're no good." The baby's autopsy came back showing microscopic myocarditis, inflammation of the heart. Very likely this baby was going to die no matter what Demetri had done, but the parents would never understand that. For months afterward, Demetri had suddenly burst into tears, and carried on, and felt sorry for himself, and practically begged people to tell him what a good doctor he was.

Cecelia had listened and patted his back and made his favorite meals for the first couple of months. But there came a day when she said, "Enough already. Learn to live with the pressures, accept them, or get out of medicine." For a while, Demetri had seriously considered taking a nice, quiet nine-to-five job where, if a brick were out of place or a ripple were left in the cement, at least no one died.

4:15 a.m. Dr. Cox sees Mrs. Coombs, an obese

hypertensive mother of six. As he enters the exam room, the doctor hears her yelling at a two-year-old in tow. "I know you're hungry. Stop crying," she says as she pulls up sharply on the small arm. The little boy looks bewildered, as if he doesn't understand.

"What can I do for you, Mrs. Coombs?" the doctor says as he pulls up a stool. She was probably pretty once, but her bone structure has disappeared into too many donuts and milkshakes.

"I've been having very bad headaches. Sometimes I see everything double."

"How long?"

"Maybe two weeks. I couldn't sleep last night because of the pain and I thought I'd come in now before I go to work."

"What kind of work do you do?"

"I clean houses."

"Do you have a doctor you see regularly?"

"No. I don't have insurance. I'm waiting to get on Medicaid."

No husband. No family support. Nothing. A world of brutalizing poverty and teenage pregnancies and mind-numbing crises, one after another. Dr. Cox prescribes Hydrodiuril to lower her blood pressure but doesn't have much faith that she will take it.

Dr. Cox drifts from the treatment room to the nurses' station where someone's made fresh popcorn. The phone rings and he hears the triage nurse say, "Sir, you need to phone for your own ambulance. We can't come to your house. Call the police and they'll give you a ride."

For a long time, Cecelia and Demetri fooled each other

with: *Love changes, settles, maybe no longer exciting, but solid, learning how to live with each other's snores and belches, the frustrating marriage instead of the perfect wedding.* Lying in bed in the darkness, Demetri had wondered what was happening to them. She didn't want him anymore.

"Are you having an affair?" Demetri asked one morning over breakfast.

"I'm not brave enough, but I wish I were."

"Why do you say that?"

"ER is your mistress, the excitement more seductive than I could ever be," Cecelia said. "How can I compete with a passion I can't argue with, or touch, or see?" And Demetri realized that Cecelia considered him unfaithful every time he left for work. He'd never been able to convince her that she was queen of his world, his wife of the sacred vows. They slept in tense shifts, like conductors carefully watching train signals to avoid crashing into each other.

Even after Cecelia told Demetri that she wanted a divorce, they tried one last time. Demetri found a special deal for a romantic week in Mexico. The vacation house, a white, peony-covered cottage with a veranda overlooking the Pacific Ocean, was on a private bay near Acapulco, one of six houses that spilled down a steep hill in a shower of bougainvillea, iguanas, stucco, red brick ledges, and lapis-lazuli swimming pools. Leaves of mango trees hung so low they nearly brushed water.

Demetri dove in, swam underwater through blazing blue so bright he could almost see through his shut eyelids. He burst to the surface, naked and clean, rising from light into the blackness of dark-green leaves. But the romantic setting felt like a rebuke. Even on vacation, Demetri heard ER voices: *Unrestrained driver trapped down on the floor. Broken femur on the right side, dislocated hip, blood pressure ninety over sixty, pulse rate one-ten.*

During the day they swam in the clear cove, and watched tropical fish browse around the underwater boulders, and sprawled together under palm-frond shelters at the beach. They wandered through open-air markets buying conch shells, and silver bracelets, and postcards to make friends at home jealous. In the evening, they sat in butterfly chairs on the terrace watching the sun light up every pink, Rubenesque curve of clouds rolling above, merging like sensuous bodies. But night brought awkward silences over drinks that got warm. They fumbled about in bed and apologized to each other afterward.

Maybe if Demetri had asked Cecelia to dance on the terrace. Maybe if he'd taken her hand and led her there. If only they'd been able to give in to the setting where every tree, every terrace, every lily said, *"This is made for romance."* The trees bordering the veranda hung motionless, heavy with moisture, their leaves theatrical shades of viridian, peacock, arsenic green. When the week was up, they were both glad to go home. The tension of wondering why they hadn't been swept away by Mexico was exhausting. At the airport, Cecelia turned to Demetri and said, "I still want a divorce."

"Are you sure?"

"I'm sure," she said as she turned to hail a cab.

What is hurting? Your arm? Are you hurting anywhere else? Your head? Try not to breathe so fast and you'll be okay.

5:30 a.m. A twenty-year-old female arrives by ambulance. Cops found cocaine in her purse and have her in cuffs.

"Don't touch me. I want to bleed everywhere. I want to bleed everywhere." She lapses into coma and it is soon apparent that she overdosed. Nurses and Dr. Cox spend forty-five minutes stabilizing her breathing and blood pressure. When she wakes up, the doctor gives her his heroin lecture.

"You are dead, you know. Shooting heroin killed you. You stopped breathing and if we hadn't been around to help you, you'd be dead."

"I didn't sign no forms and I'm suing for malpractice right now," she whispers.

Now, as a ten-year veteran of the doctor wars, sometimes when Demetri Cox joins the circle of doctors and nurses standing around an ER patient with tubes in every orifice, unable to speak around bits of plastic, the target of all modern science's magical power, he gets flashbacks of his group of first-year students as they gingerly encircled their cadaver. *There's a 420-pound cardiac arrest in Room 4. He should count as two arrests,* was a standard joke. A curtain of silence fell around the cadaver experience. No one was supposed to show that it affected them. Walking down Denver streets, sometimes Dr. Cox catches himself feeling like a body among bodies, rather than a person among people. *How did you get your burn? Were you drinking? I'll have the nurse give you a little medicine to help you calm down.*

"Dr. Cox, your wife left this letter for you," a nurse says as she hands him an envelope. Demetri recognizes Cecelia's neat handwriting. He tosses the envelope from one hand to the other, as if it were too hot to touch. The only quiet place is in the linen closet. He leans his back against a wall and reads her letter, then crumbles the paper in his hands.

If only flesh became something like granite burning with mineral fire. If only a severed limb remained as a column of marble, a dazzle of sparkling beauty independent of time. If the body were some iridescent substance, hard and cold as ice, ruby heart, diamond brain inexhaustible, impervious, then he could walk the world seeing everything, knowing everything, needing nothing, no one. But no one is made of granite or ice.

Better than almost anyone else, Demetri Cox knows human beings are ligaments and synapses and blood cells. All he's been left with is the tacky skin of words. Good-bye words, good-riddance phrases, the disorientation when the clumsy tongue is finally free. How to sing a new self without words at all. Like a snake discards the skins of past lives, sleek, unimpeded. If only he lived in a world where milk was the only food anyone ever needed, and there were breasts enough for everyone. A world in which everyone was promised that health and love would never dissolve. But, like the passage from Borges that Cecelia used to read to Demetri, *Love is a religion with a fallible god.*

8 a.m. Demetri tightens his seatbelt, drives towards home through the smell of heavy summer rain falling on grass and pines. Denver streets untangle into junctions,

squares, cul-de-sacs. Kids stand in line for the school bus. A woman in the car in front of him strains to apply lipstick while she drives. Orange lamps lead him towards home. Demetri turns on the radio to the jazz station: "Baby, be good to me, you don't have to cry no more." Blood clings to the cuffs of his pants, the soles of his shoes. He pulls into his parking spot in front of the apartment house, opens the car door and catches his face in the rearview mirror: eyes burn, the skin over his cheeks is dry, puffy. Mouth tastes like burnt coffee.

After Demetri shuts the apartment door, there is a remarkable stillness. Like a room where someone is lying dead. He stands there listening, expecting something to happen. Cecelia has taken the bookcase with all her books, the walnut dining table, the chairs she so painstakingly refinished. Nothing of her is left, not the dishes, the vacuum sweeper, the pottery vase they bought in Mexico. Only things that aren't remain: tree shadows, the ghost of leaves.

Demetri sleeps with the lights on, as if Cecelia might still be coming home, turns on the radio the moment he enters the apartment. Fluffs of dust scatter as he walks through to the bedroom.

Even when he closes his eyes, he sees scenes from the emergency room. Shouts. Curses. Shrieks of curtain hooks on steel rods. Hands all over bodies. Medicine's probing, struggle for control, everything shifting. Even in the midst of ER patients coming and going, and Cecelia settling into her new apartment across town, the moon, quite steady and white and glowing, shines down on everything. *Please sir, lie still. I'm going to numb you now. Hang on, man. Soon the pain will be gone.*

THE ISOLATION ROOM

". . . and the room was the most absolutely silent place I
have ever been."

— The Plutonium Files,
Eileen Welsome

There is the smell of green soap, the low rumble of
voices as Mary walks through the gray hallway. Sitting in
the small wing chair across from Dr. Lang, she struggles
to explain her actions to this earnest man in the white
jacket.

"You have to let me out of here. This is all a big
mistake," Mary says as she pulls down the sleeves of her
blue sweater, hiding the bandage on her left wrist. She is
tall and brown-haired and wiry.

"You'll be with us for at least seventy-two hours. How
was cutting your wrist an accident?" the doctor asks, pen
poised above Mary's chart. His neck and bald head are
brown from many afternoons on golf greens. Gray

sprinkles the short brown hair at his temples.

"I was chopping carrots for stew and Tom called me from the living room and I turned around to answer him, and when I turned back, my wrist was bleeding."

"Your husband thinks you need help. He says you've been talking when no one else is in the room. Who were you talking to?" Dr. Lang asks.

"The characters in my novel," Mary whispers. She has no words to explain how the man with a large leather hat and camera slung around his neck had shown up in her tiny room carved out under the eaves.

"Hello. Is it you?" "Yes, it's me." "Are you ready to listen?" "Yes." "Then follow me." Mary had no choice but to obey. Cameron was a photographer who documented the landscape along the Oregon coast, a place that used to have fish. Now there was a nuclear reactor grey against the horizon. Of course, her hero fell in love, and had to survive pneumonia, and the sinking of his boat.

"Do you hear them talking to you?" Dr. Lang looks up from his writing. Mary has his complete attention now. He looks every bit as anxious as Mary feels, but she's the one in the hospital costume of one-size-fits-all khaki shirt and pants.

"I don't exactly *hear* them. It's more like they become so real that I *know* what they're going to say," Mary says.

Big Nurse sticks her head inside the door. "You have to come quick, Dr. Lang," she sputters.

"What is it?"

"Susan started a fire in the dayroom."

Big Nurse is a tense, gangly woman with doughy skin and deep crow's feet by both eyes. As the doctor lurches for the door, Mary tags along behind. Full of noise and milling, the place smells like disinfectant and smoke. Card tables are scattered around the dayroom. Men and women pace. The emotional temperature in the room is running high. A radio shouts from the corner. Vinyl chairs are scarred with burns. The room is full of high-pitched tones, men and women, staring, swaying. A tiny woman with blonde hair sits hunched in the corner of the room, her face that of a survivor walking away from a car accident without memory. Her breasts and hips are mere bumps within her blue hospital dress. A newspaper on a small table is ablaze.

The nurse pulls the pin on the fire extinguisher and sprays white foam. A circle of eyes hover on the perimeter. Dr. Lang lifts his right hand. Three male staff members close in. Susan snorts and swears as they pin her legs and arms.

"No one is trying to hurt you. If you stop fighting, we'll let you up," Dr. Lang says. "Nurse, give her the sedative I ordered." A shot to her buttock and Susan is carried into the isolation room. Exhaustion wins out over struggle. She lies in her gown, ankles and wrists secured in leather cuffs strapped to the bed frame. The room is eight-feet long, eight-feet wide, ten-feet high. Mary watches as the steel door, with only a judas window to peek through, is closed. An old woman with white hair and eyes that know everything starts to cackle.

"Mary, shall we continue?" Dr. Lang ushers her back into his office. Sun makes a rainbow on the wall. He crosses to the window and closes the blinds. "Why did you drop out of graduate school?" He settles in once again behind his desk, pen poised to take down her story.

"My creative thesis was rejected. My professor said my

fiction was too surrealistic to be approved by the thesis committee. I think his exact words were 'too bleak, not believable.' He accused me of getting too carried away with my own imagination."

Mary was a woman who had always believed in signs, but the day of her accident she had paid no mind to how icy clouds fell across the sun, how her mouth tasted like metal. Mary had stood at the kitchen counter thinking about whether her hero and heroine should adopt a second child. She was chopping beef into small cubes for the stew. Then her wrist was bleeding. One instant was all it took. She was still cleaning up the mess when Tom walked in.

"So, you've finally done it."

"It was an accident."

"Tell that to your doctor," Tom had yelled. "Come on. I'm driving you to the Emergency Room." The ER doctor had called Dr. Lang, the psychiatrist on call, who admitted Mary on a seventy-two-hour hold. Now there was no way out except through the court system. Tom had said that she was out of her mind so many times maybe it wasn't really as negative as she'd first believed. Maybe to be out of her mind meant she'd made the leap from logical to intuitive, into her true skin, a room all her own. What rearrangement of brain cells, chemical imbalance ever made her think she could be a writer, that teller of lies, pursuer of truth by means other than logical, that follower of breadcrumbs through the scary forest wherever they lead?

Pills, Ladies," Big Nurse shouts as she calls out names,

one after the other, orders them to take their medicine while she watches. Red pills. Green pills. Orange pills. Blue pills. More colors than a box of crayons. Big Nurse hands out experimental pills that still don't have names: SKD Laboratories X-233.

"Mary Simons," she calls. "Swallow this."

"What is it?"

"Your medicine." Mary swallows. There's nothing else she can do in this bone-house. Soul-cemetery. Through the window are green fields, long hilly roads. The windows in the dayroom slide open only three inches. *No visitors. No telephone. No exit.* There is a great emphasis on being "good." The day's lassitude continues. The numbing before television, the hours with television, the hours after television. The usual topics that Mary used to write about— sex, violence, abuse, corruption of power—have been preempted by the six o'clock news. The medicine makes her feel groggy, dizzy, faint. Her muscles become rigid, twitchy. Sunlight glancing off the windowpane, the red-white-blue flag flying on the pole outside seems dull.

Vivaldi or Muzak on the radio; it makes no difference. Mary sits in the corner staring at her hands. She has nothing to say, no small talk, no anecdotes. Gone are the days of wearing nail polish with names like Tangerine Sunset, Mist On The Moors, Bronze Mardi Gras. No more listening to Janis Joplin: *"Freedom's just another word for nothing left to lose..."* She wrote to get to know Cameron Dunlap, to follow close behind while he photographed the Oregon coast. *Why does this shoreline look so naked? What is happening to this landscape?*

Mary fished her hero out of the river after his boat tipped over and heard the voice she slowly recognized as her own in an attempt to save the only life she could save. The images and dialogue that showed up on paper were rarely as good as the writing in her head. A state of anxiety was Mary's natural habitat. The landscape of the human brain, gaunt and jagged, was also breathtaking.

Another gray morning. Overnight the reds and golds are gone. The Blue Spruce outside is snow-whelmed. Mary awakens to this white world as nurses bustle around making beds.

Mary troops along with everyone else, in single file, to the dayroom, surrounded by facial tics and word salads. The air weighs too much, like an airport in bad weather. Today, God is a bigamist because two women on the ward claim Him as husband. Susan is out of isolation, sits on a low stool in a corner rubbing her crotch, looking around, moving her lips. She is drugged to the point of muteness. Mary sits down next to her.

"It must feel good to be out of isolation," Mary says as a way of breaking the silence. "Are you hearing voices?" What if there were something on the other side of crazy, a new understanding across that line, a special knowledge?

"I can hear Nora and Annabelle very clearly," Susan whispers. Her face has grown pasty from waiting for nothing.

"Do you hear Susan's voice?" Mary asks.

"No. Susan is dead. Nora and Anabelle are here."

"Am I talking to Nora now?"

"No, you've got Anabelle now," Susan whispers, as if it were a secret.

"Can you tell me who Nora and Anabelle are?"

"They came when Susan was killed. Susan had to be

killed because she was very bad." Susan gazes off into a landscape only she can see and starts moving her hand in her crotch again.

"Please don't do that," Mary says as she throws a pillow over her. It's still obvious what she's doing. Susan slaps her own hand.

"Nora does that to Anabelle all the time," Susan says, lost somewhere in the crowd.

"Are you hungry? It's time for lunch," Mary says. The mess hall is a large room filled with long tables in three separate rows with plastic chairs. Only here a day, Mary has learned the rules for survival: *Be first in line for food or you may not get any. Never stand or sit anywhere without your back to the wall. Never make a fast move in someone's direction.*

"Nora is but Anabelle isn't," Susan says. Mary brings her a tray and watches as Susan divides everything in two sections, the potatoes, the beef, the peaches. *"Don't let me end up like her,"* Mary says to no one in particular.

The dayroom walls are painted industrial blue. A man jogs determinedly around the nurses' station. Big Nurse stands at the corner of his route and manages a two- or three-sentence exchange per circuit.

"How long has Susan been here?" Mary asks as the nurse jangles the keys to the front door, the staff bathroom, the restraint key that looks like a pocketknife— silver, pointed.

"She came to us six years ago. A severe depression after the birth of her second child."

"Six years. Do any women go home from here?" Mary watches the ever-moving line of chattering patients in a hurry to go nowhere.

"Some," the nurse says.

"Tell Dr. Lang I need to see him," Mary says.

"Won't do any good. You're with us until your hearing."

"What hearing?"

"A competency hearing," the nurse says as casually as if she were talking about the dinner menu.

"May I make a phone call? I need to call my husband."

"Tomorrow. Just behave yourself today and we'll see."

The phone is between the dayroom and the dormitory and Mary could go and pick it up except it's connected to a switchboard on another ward and has no dial. *If only I could make Tom understand, he'll forgive me. He is the one who put me here. He is the one who kept saying, "you are wild, you are wacko, you are high as a kite."*

When still in her teens, Mary had written in her journal a list of things she feared: recitation at the front of the class, germs on the counter, dark at the top of the stairs, boys, the future, and knowing that whatever she did would never be good enough. At a young age, Mary dealt with her fears by turning them into word pictures, edgy prose that said, *see, it's manageable, you can deal with this.*

When Mary was in her twenties, she fell in love with Dean, the hero in Jack Kerouac's novel, *On The Road*. Actually, she wanted to *be* him more than *have* him. *"For to him sex was the one and holy thing in life…"* But of course that novel was a lie: it equated youth with liberty and youth for Mary had meant curfews and rejection slips. They met when she was jogging along a path in Washington Park when Tom ran his bike into her. "Sorry," he had said as he helped her up. "The sun was in my eyes."

His knees were brown, cheeks brown, and Mary had guessed that he was brown under his shorts too.

"Let me get a cab. I'll take you to ER to make sure you're okay," Tom had said.

Hungry people make poor shoppers, was one of her mother's favorite sayings. Mary was starving. It was Tom's thumb-in-the-nose attitude towards his parents and politics and society in general that had first attracted her. He moved as though there were water under his skin instead of muscle. *All you need is love*, sang the Beatles.

Mary and Tom were part of an eighties resurgence of love-ins, incense and beads, psychedelic fashions of flowered pants and colorful robes, hearts painted on foreheads. *Peace and Love. Turn on, tune in. Make love not war.* Love, that only socially acceptable psychosis.

Behind closed doors, their couches leaked stuffing, drapes were grey and torn, appliances were in a continual state of breakdown. Tom would only let her buy brown towels and sheets. He made erratic and unpredictable appearances at home, demanding to be fed. On car trips, Tom refused to stop for bathroom breaks or food.

"And here's a man who gives thousands of dollars every year to the Humane Society and the Red Cross," Mary tells Dr. Lang.

"Have you told anyone before now?" Dr. Lang asks.

"No one would believe me," she says.

"I believe you. Does he hit you?"

"No. It's all threats. And violent outbursts. When a burglar broke into our apartment on Capitol Hill, Tom bought a gun. At first, he carried it in the glove compartment of his jeep. Then it migrated to our bedside table. When he decided to go to the police academy, he started carrying it in his pocket. *Why are you so angry?"* Tom would say. *Don't you ever see the pollution and the people on street corners sleeping in boxes?* I'd say. *I can't do anything about it,* Tom told me. *You're right. You have to see what's going on before you can do anything to change it,* I insisted."

Mary tells Dr. Lang her story the only way she knows how.

For a second the door is open. Those patients with passes file out. Two women scuffle and, in the confusion and noise, Mary mingles in, her ticket to walk. She's out the door. *Walk, don't run. Find the gate.* She follows the road, past the frozen creek, the pristine lawn that the public sees. Away from the view of back wards behind her, nighttime screams. Away from restraints and being treated like a piece of furniture, a social zero. The odor of cheap food and poor washing. Past the administration building, the petunia beds shriveled from frost, Dr. Lang's private residence. *Keep walking.* A cloud of starlings swoop and dive. Mary is on the road now. Through the trees, she can see a church steeple and aims in that direction.

A car roars up beside her, full of *them.* Big Nurse and a technician in green scrubs and bulging muscles. They try to tackle Mary. She doesn't resist. "I'm not escaping. I'm going for a walk," Mary protests. "There's no need to hurt my arm."

"Leaving is against the law," the nurse says from the front seat. When Mary gets back to the hospital, a nurse pokes her with a needle fast, like a bee sting. *I will grow old here. My face framed in the window unseen. I'll become one of the night fliers, a little old lady floating around on the wings of my pills*. Now she is merry, but not too merry. She asks Big Nurse about her life, admires, is good-natured, once again a child who had just decided to go for a walk. Crazy is a different point of view, a different circle of the Inferno, being stuck in this unexpected twist in the plot. Collapse, agree to be crazy, surrender, withdraw.

Mary's writing room was in the attic, books and newspapers piled along the wall. First there had to be quality staring-out-the-window time. One cup of coffee. One lit white candle. Her favorite black fine-pointed pen. Then she would begin: *Summer burned hot on the New Mexico prairie. Morning slipped by and still there was no sound of birdsong. A breeze. Nothing more.*

Where were the meadowlarks? The scissortail flycatchers?..."

"Have you seen this newspaper article?" she had said, as she thrust an article at Tom. "Frogs were found dead in the South Platte River. Why aren't people upset about this? It's frogs first and people next," Mary had ranted.

"Chill out," Tom had mumbled under his breath as he walked out of the room. Mary had retreated to her room in the attic where she felt safe and understood by the characters in her novel.

"Walking away was a stupid thing to do, Mary," Dr. Lang says. "Your illness is a special room you've invented in order to live in an unlivable situation. Ontological insecurity," Dr. Lang says. Mary laughs and considers trying to explain the lives of Anne Sexton or Sylvia Plath to her doctor but decides it would be useless. Mary can tell that Dr. Lang thinks her laughter is inappropriate.

"You can't keep me here. The nurse says I'm going to have a competency trial. Why didn't you tell me? When is it?"

"Next Monday."

"Mental illness is a label you doctors have invented to conceal conflict as illness, to justify coercion as treatment," Mary says.

"Tell that to the judge. I'm trying to help," Dr. Lang says.

"I'd rather find my own way."

Mary has the same feeling in the pit of her stomach that she did on the day of her oral exam on John Milton's *Paradise Lost*. She had panicked because she couldn't remember whether Milton had put the sun or the earth at the center of the universe. During class, Mary's mind had recorded how the dust on the windows refracted amber light on classroom walls, how the radiators sounded like castanets, how the neck of the man sitting in front of her was leaning forward like a reed. Now all Mary hears from Dr. Lang, just as she'd heard from Professor Slade, was who she was not. She keeps struggling to discover who she is.

When Professor Slade's book of poetry, *Saigon Primer*, was published, Mary had tried to engage her thesis advisor in a discussion of his book. At the publication party, there were copies of *Poetry* strewn on the table carrying reviews that claimed his book was "daring," "provocative," "complex."

"Are you using the hand grenades as metaphors for the emotional turmoil in the soldiers?" Mary had asked while sipping her Chablis.

"You missed the point, my dear," Professor Slade had said in his condescending tone.

Mary had called fog 'fog' and was told that she was the one with the foggy brain. Mary had retreated to her writing room to say what she meant, to describe what she saw. Too late she understood how dangerous clear vision could be.

Tom had committed her to this hospital with certificates from two physicians proclaiming she was insane. No questions asked. "Get dressed for your ride," Tom had said.

"You can't imprison me without a trial," Mary had protested.

"It's for your own protection."

"Don't I have a right to my own opinion?"

"Only if you think right."

"You mean like you," Mary had said.

After leaving university, Mary had thought, *Okay, they think I'm a surrealistic writer. I'll give them surrealism. What is the most bizarre thing our government could do to its citizens? What is the worst thing one human could inject into another?* Plutonium. That purplish liquid that gives off an eerie animal-like warmth when concentrated in small amounts. Plutonium, the 94th element with a half-life of 86 years. Named after the small planet, Pluto, the Greek god of the Underworld. Deaf to prayers. Unmoved by sacrifices.

The protagonist of her novel was a doctor who worked for the Los Alamos Project, creators of the atomic bomb:

When the doctor stepped off the train in New Mexico, the light was intoxicating. Vast distances glittered like the bottom of a primeval sea. Blue mountains floated on the rim of the horizon. Here the skin of the world felt so thin it seemed that a bigger reality was about to break through. Dr. Tallwood wore the wrinkled suit, tie, clean white shirt that was his uniform. He dreamed of unlocking the secrets of the human body. Find a cure for cancer maybe.

"All we need to do is give a tracer dose of radioactive substance and follow its path with a Geiger counter. It's possible to uncover blockages in the circulatory system," he said. He had discovered a magic bullet that would strike straight at disease. Carefully Dr. Tallwood selected eleven patients. Each was injected with five micrograms of plutonium. Each was assigned the initials "HP" plus a number. Each person became a "Human Product" to be studied. None of the patients gave consent for what was being given to them.

Saul was tired from a long week working as a cement mixer. Cataracts made his view of the world cloudy blue. At 6:30 one morning in July, Saul drove up to the construction site. He never saw the dump truck barreling straight towards him. It was too late to turn, too late to brake.

He was admitted to the army hospital, assigned to Dr. Tallwood's care, with fractures of both femurs but otherwise in good health. A week later Dr. Tallwood mixed a plutonium cocktail into a syringe and injected it into Saul's arm. Forever after in his medical records Saul was referred to as HP-12 and became part of a secret war of invisible toxins and government cover-up, a forgotten guinea pig.

Mary follows Susan into the line forming for breakfast.

Susan hops from one foot to the other. People scatter like roaches as she runs towards them. Big Nurse jangles her keys, letting everyone know who's boss. The new nurse frantically tries to pull up the trousers of a woman who streaks across the room. An old lady paces, fritters nervously with her hands. She turns and swats a young girl who walks disdainfully away. The old lady lunges. There is the sound of flesh hitting flesh. Big Nurse runs to referee. Mary feels damp and stained.

After breakfast, Mary puts on the black skirt and white blouse that Tom brought. She takes special care with her lipstick, pinches her cheeks to give her face color. At the head of the table sits a black-robed judge. On one side, a battery of doctors and an assistant state Attorney General congregate. Mary sits opposite them, patiently waiting to ask for her freedom.

Dr. Lang begins, "The essential feature of delusional disorder is the presence of one or more non-bizarre delusions that persist for at least one month, situations that can conceivably occur in real life, like being poisoned or infected or loved from a distance."

"Where is my representative, my voice?" Mary whispers to Big Nurse.

"Dr. Lang will speak on your behalf," she says.

"But he's the one who wants to keep me here," Mary protests. "I want to speak for myself."

"It won't do any good," Big Nurse mumbles, but leans over to tell Dr. Lang. Mary feels all the eyes judging her facial expression, her gait as she climbs the stand, pulls her sweater more tightly around her shoulders.

"I sit before you because of an accident I had with a knife. I am not crazy. Dr. Lang insists that I'm a danger to myself. He is keeping me here without my consent. Does he value my life more than I do? I must be allowed freedom in order to do my work. He's even taken away my pen."

"Dr. Lang is acting in your best interests."

"How do you know that? If one of his patients were suicidal because he'd lost all his money, would Dr. Lang give him *his* money? Or if a patient doesn't want to live because he's alone in the world, would Dr. Lang offer him *his* friendship? I don't think so. I'm being punished for expressing anger. Don't you see what's happening in the world? What gives you the right to dictate how I feel? No one can tell me what mental illness is and what it is not."

"That is a problem," Dr. Lang admits.

"To say that mental illness is nothing but disease is like saying that an opera is nothing but musical notes. You are punishing me for daring to have a different thought system. For not obeying commands quickly enough. Who owns my life? Me? The state? My husband?"

"You're here because you harmed yourself."

"I've told you. That was an accident."

"What evidence do you have, Dr. Lang, to support your continuing treatment of Mrs. Simons?" the Judge asks.

"Her husband has brought in her notebooks. She needs further observation. She has page after page of notes about how doctors working for our government injected unsuspecting patients with plutonium," Dr. Lang says.

"Isn't that what they use in making bombs?" the Judge asks. "Yes."

"But that really happened," Mary says. "You can accuse me of not turning all the information I've researched into a good story if you want, but you can't tell me I'm suffering from delusions. This really happened. I have proof."

"May I approach the bench? Judge," Dr. Lang asks. Their heads almost touch as they whisper. The walnut clock chimes three o'clock. Mary knows it's now or never.

"Men want crops without plowing ground. They want rain without thunder and lightning. Want the ocean without the awful roar of its water," Mary says slowly, careful not to show anger. "And you think I'm the one who's crazy?"

Night is a parallel universe. Moon on snow. The lights in the dorm are out. Susan, lying in the bed next to Mary, cries out in her sleep. A woman at the end of the room is softly weeping. All Mary wants is to be in her room under the eaves where she heard messages in the wind, then silence. Where grass was gentle breath, a hush. "Here's to freedom," Mary whispers, "its glimmering then dimming out like lightning bugs squeezed between two fingers." She watches snow fall, the yellowed swirl at the corner streetlight, the quick flakes banking on the windowsill, covering distant evergreens. Morning comes without Mary having even closed her eyes. She dresses and waits in a chair outside the doctor's office.

"I'm going to release you today," Dr. Lang says as he shuts the door to his office.

"You are?" Mary says, with a mixture of fear and relief passing through her body. "Have you told Tom?"

"No. I wanted to talk to you first. This discharge is contingent on your remaining on your medications and continuing regular therapy sessions. Will you agree to ongoing treatment?"

"Yes. I do feel better. I'm going to tell Tom that I need

time to myself, rent an apartment," Mary says. "Feeling safe and protected has helped me understand how stressful my marriage has been. Thank you, Dr. Lang." Dr. Lang crosses the room to shake her hand. In this austere place, with its locked doors and desolate hallways, no knife could accidentally slip. Seclusion and time are the real healers, this hospital a kinder, gentler madhouse than the world outside.

Maybe the slip of that knife was no accident at all.

TESTAMENT

Laura walks down the long hall as silent call lights flash and muffled voices sift under closed doors. As she enters her patient's room, the air smells of soap and urine and roses that someone forgot to throw out. The old man, yellow and gaunt, is crumpled into a ball facing the wall. At first Laura thinks that he must be sleeping, undoubtedly worn out from his safari over the side rails, into the jungle of chairs and overbed tables and wastepaper baskets. His eyelids open and quickly close. The old man is watching her from beneath his hooded eyelids, his face a death mask.

"Good morning, Mr. Lewis."

"Morning... borning... blarney," he says. Cachexia is a word that Laura has just learned, the medical phrase for the jut of his facial bones, the too-hot glow in his eyes, caused by anemia maybe, or a cancer they've not yet detected. The word could just as well describe some exotic dance or cult or religion.

As Laura sets the pack of clean linen on the straight-backed vinyl chair, her hands tremble. In report, Jackson, the night nurse, had said that Mr. Lewis had managed to get out of two restraints and climbed over the side rail. A regular Houdini. On her six a.m. rounds, Jackson found him sitting in the middle of the floor, a nude cross-legged guru, humming a mantra known only to himself, eyes fixed on some deity on the ceiling. A trail of diarrhea and urine smeared the floor.

"It's a miracle that there were no broken bones," Jackson had sighed wearily, pulling her white sweater around her thin frame. "We picked him up and got him back into bed. I was congratulating myself that none of it had gotten on my uniform and then I looked down. My pant cuff was brown. He's had a quick bath, but probably will need another one before breakfast."

Laura walks to the window and pulls open the curtains. The sun is just coming up and shoots prisms of red, and blue, and green, as if through a stained-glass window, spheres wheeling within spheres, man and woman, saint and sinner seen through a thousand facets of glass. From the street far below, there is the belching of engines, the pounding of a jackhammer. An ambulance speeds for a birth or a death that will be tucked into tomorrow's newspaper between the stock exchange listings and weddings. When she turns to look at Mr. Lewis, his legs are flailing air, as if he were scrambling up a ladder, a stationary bicycle taking him nowhere.

It is Laura's first month of training as a nurse, a novitiate, a lark, a darling eager to heal. Her profile is firm young bone with no fatty deposits anywhere. She still must earn that badge of knowledge that comes when fingers become eyes seeing the illusive vein, a relief map guiding the needle to the intricate canal system flowing under muscle and skin. She has never given a man a bath before. How do you wash arms and hairy chests and legs without exposing a man's privates? An innocent who still believes in healing by the laying on of a cool palm.

"I'm going to help you get washed up for breakfast, Mr. Lewis." She bustles around the room, whisking washbasin from nightstand, turns her back to him as fine mist clouds the mirror.

Sometimes when Laura looks through the glass of a store window, she sees her father watching her. He was pastor of the Bethany Baptist Church. Laura had grown up listening to her father cajole, inspire, preach about the meaning of life. Laura had sat every Sunday in the third pew, left side, directly in front of her father's pulpit as he preached about the Fall, incarnation, resurrection, blood atonement, heaven and hell. Raising Lazarus from the dead. World created in six days. Demons, the cause of illness and madness.

Laura was sixteen when she stopped going to church because, if what her father preached were true, that God is responsible for everything that happens on earth, she wanted no part of Him. God, the Great Accountant, the Cold-Eyed Leveler, the one who keeps the books balanced. The belief that for every precious gift received, something equally precious will be taken away. Either-Or. Black or white. Saved or doomed to a fiery inferno. Little baby in the manger. Dead Jew on the Cross. Inerrancy of the Bible. Good News, God Spell, words from which the word 'Gospel' springs.

"All the gospels share so much in common, say almost

the same thing. Why?" Laura had asked her father.

"They may have all come from the same source, the "O" source. We'll never know. But it doesn't matter. Don't ever expect to see the results of your work," he'd told Laura. "Hope is the single most important ingredient for changing the world, and that's what we're losing now." She watched him orchestrate meetings between pastors and lay church leaders to help find shelter for the homeless. Set up health clinics for the working poor.

"It's easy to love Mankind in the abstract, but it's a lot harder to love a specific person," her father had said. A picture hung in their living room of her father being led away in handcuffs from the Capitol Rotunda. His crime was mounting a protest without official approval.

"I'm embarrassed by the things we humans do in God's name. I'm leaving the ministry because religion has become a sword that divides, rather than a balm that heals," he'd said. The church Deacons asked him to leave because he was spending too much time visiting prison inmates, taking soup to the homeless on Denver streets. For having bumper stickers on his Datsun: "Dissent is patriotic;" "War is terrorism with a bigger budget." Her father preached agape while dealing out totalitarian discipline in their home. Laura never knew exactly when the bottle of gin crept into his desk drawer, but once it got there, it never left.

She grew up hearing her father preach about the New Testament. Old Testament. How the Bible had changed from papyrus to printed page to digital. Perennial. Ageless. *"In the beginning was the word..."*

"Human nature doesn't change, from the seduction by Delilah, to the betrayal by Judas, to Job lamenting his boils," her father had whispered.

"But there has to be an answer," Laura had insisted. "Who decided which books were to be included or excluded in the Bible? Why were the Apocrypha, Judith, the Maccabees left out? Who decided when the Bible was sealed and sent out into the world? The alphabet and the hand of man were used in the process. How do we know that God was there?"

Later she went with her father to AA meetings, which were like a perverse church service with their ritualistic structure of repeated phrases, where a deity was invoked. But here alcohol was God. Sinners offered personal testimonials about the power of God, described their encounters with God Alcohol, joked about God Alcohol, recited collective prayers to appease God Alcohol. *Count Your Blessings. One Day at A Time. Live and Let Live.* Plain speech made the familiar vivid, personal, immediate. Here concreteness was king: the brand of booze, the names of bars, what wives said to husbands during the last fight, what the cop looked like when the sinner landed in the slammer.

After her father's stroke, the left side of his mouth drooped, giving him a perpetual sneer. Sometimes when Laura looks in the bathroom mirror, her father's eyes slip into hers. Same shade of cobalt blue. Same crinkle at the corners. It's so real that sometimes Laura talks to him, but he doesn't answer. If she tries to get too close, he disappears.

Gently Laura places the soft bath blanket over Mr. Lewis' body. Miss Bradley had picked up the arm of Harry, the mannequin, all the while explaining the correct technique of applying wet soapy cloth, lotion.

"Brisk movement improves circulation," she'd said while holding the mannequin's left arm between her thumb and forefinger, as far from her starched uniform as possible. Laura had taken a turn with Harry but didn't need to worry about what the person in the bed might be thinking, or that she'd have to keep up her end of the conversation.

"When can I go home?" Mr. Lewis whispers. "Will you help me go home?" Mr. Lewis fingers a Kleenex, folding, unfolding, shredding it into fine confetti. He leans towards Laura and holds up the tattered remains. "Look," he says, "pretty!"

Laura snatches the paper from his hands. "Please lie still. I'm trying to give you a bath." Lewis is quiet for a while, perhaps as long as two minutes. And then he begins to rock forward and back, farther and farther, until his face touches his bent knees. Laura dips the washcloth into warm water, rubs the soap across it, folds the cloth around her hand the way Miss Bradley taught. She washes his face, gently around the eyes, the chin.

"They laughed at Bell.... They laughed at Edison.... I'm a doctor, you know. I'm glad to be a patient... it makes me humble.... Oral Roberts came to visit me last night...."

As Laura washes his other arm and chest, Lewis looks at a spot above her head. His hands keep worrying the cloth restraints, his ropey muscles straining, as if he were fingering a rosary.

"Jesus told me he was born two thousand years ago... he says I can call him J.C.... I have cancer of the nerves... mental telepathy...."

Before his stroke, Laura's father used to be a champ at word games. He was a great reader, lover of crossword puzzles, the English language. The sound of words. The playful meaning of words. One day at Aunt Cora's house, he and Laura were talking about witchcraft. He kept looking up the word for Satan. Laura came up with words like "Beelzebub" and "Lucifer." Her father had said "demon," but there was another word that he couldn't think of. He kept saying "dev-den... dev-den."

"Don't you mean 'devil,' Father?" Laura cut his steak into small pieces, mashed his baked potato. He only had use of his right hand.

She rinses the washcloth, soaps it again, drapes the bath blanket carefully, exposing the old man's right leg. Lewis' voice was moist, as there were bubbles in his throat through which words must slowly rise.

"Let me up on the stage."

"What stage, Mr. Lewis?"

"Up there... where people are being healed... the man just took off his brace."

"Where do you think you are?"

"Why, in the auditorium... people are coming... in wheelchairs...."

"You're in the hospital. Remember?" Breakfast trays rattle down the hall outside.

Laura is done now except for "finishing the bath," the euphemism Miss Bradley used for washing a patient's genitals. "Always ask the patient if he can 'finish his bath,'" Miss Bradley had said.

"Mr. Lewis, here is the washcloth. You can finish your bath now. I'll be back in a moment."

"It's snowing... see... it's snowing."

"No, it's just your tissue... that you keep tearing in pieces... please... finish your bath."

He kicks his right leg, then his left. Kicks off the bath blanket and there he lies naked, his penis a shrunken sinew in the hollow of his thigh. Laura's father had loved the origin of words, had told her that words like "testament," "testify," "testimony," began from oaths sworn by ancient men on their testicles. Abraham's servant had sworn by placing his hand under the thigh of his master. Zeus made Dionysus come forth from his father's thigh. "If a woman grabs a man's privates, her hand must be cut off," her father whispered.

Laura soaks the washcloth in warm water, makes it slick with soap. She washes Mr. Lewis between his legs. It's not difficult. He pays her no mind. As she looks into his eyes, it is her father she is washing, his arms, thin barrel chest, his hands with their endless shake, shake, shake, hands that would never make a fist again, never grip a hammer, shovel, or pick.

"Wherever I go, I take myself with me. That always spoils it," Lewis says. His remark is silly, innocent. Of no more significance than a breeze coming up out of nowhere. A yellow haze on a day that is strangely still. Laura laughs in spite of herself. Lewis laughs like a mechanical face in a funhouse—bobbing and shrieking its ha-ha-ha on a deserted sidewalk. He has no teeth. All at once he becomes serious.

"Saint Hildegard was right," Lewis says solemnly.

"She was? What did she say?" Laura asks, fastening his clean gown in the back.

"God does not inhabit healthy bodies," he whispers, closing his eyes.

"See you later," Laura says as she tucks the blanket around his legs.

"I hope so," the old man smiles. He reaches out two bony arms and touches her softly on the shoulders. He is healing her now.

SPECIAL NEEDS

Maria spreads the blue pamphlet on the top of the toilet, holds her breath while she reads instructions, pulls the home pregnancy test out of its cardboard box. *Please let it be a false alarm. Only a missed period.* She sees the color change. There in her hands is proof that she can never get away with anything. Ever. "Damn you, Randall," she says, then adds, "Sorry, Mom," looking around as if her mother were standing behind her in the stall. Shame is a Catholic thing. Birth out of wedlock is sin with a capital "S."

She buries the evidence in the bottom of the wastebasket, straightens her short black skirt and heads to work. She puts on her big grin, server skin, and brings iced tea and catsup and to-go boxes for the diners at Creekside. Dishes clatter. Children run amok. She wants to say, "Why can't you people feed yourself?" but what she actually says is, "Can I get you anything else?" What Maria likes about waitressing the most is there's never much time to think.

It's so hot in the restaurant that Maria's blonde hair frizzes, her face tingles as if it's about to break out in a rash. Someone has put money in the jukebox and Bonnie Raitt is singing "The Road's My Middle Name." Maria takes orders at her six tables, repeats them to Al in the kitchen, tells Betty what beverages to prepare, tallies up bills, hands back change, thanks regulars for generous tips, all the while thinking: *What am I going to do?*

"Phone, Maria," Al calls from the kitchen.

"This is Diane Bradley at Westview. I'm calling about your brother. He's organizing a protest. Insists that the patients should be allowed to live on the outside." Maria finishes her shift and heads out to the institution where Tommy lives.

"Don't you ever get tired of watching that?" Maria asks, throwing her coat on the back of her brother's wheelchair, huddled with the others. All eyes are riveted to the black box that is their primary connection to the outside world of politics and civil rights and romantic possibilities. Their hero is Ironside, Raymond Burr, rolling along in his wheelchair while his secretary-sidekick follows behind.

"I'm like him," Tommy says, trying for a high five but missing. "He got shot and is in a wheelchair like me. Everybody wants to feel sorry for him, but he doesn't want pity. He wants to take care of himself. Like me." Tommy has the curved nose of a patrician, prominent cheekbones. Deeply set robin-egg blue eyes, endearing in their innocence. Sometimes when they talk, Maria ends up looking into the whites of his eyes.

"You're more handsome," Maria says, kissing him on

the cheek. "Come on, let's go to your room. I need to talk to you." She pushes his wheelchair down the long corridor. A saxophone doo-wops down the hall. "Diane called me. What's this I hear about you organizing a protest?"

"I want an apartment so that I can live with Sophie," Tommy says before Maria can even sit down. They've had this conversation before. With difficulty, he pulls papers out of a folder on his desk. "See, I've got it all written down. Our government is spending almost $500.00 a day each for Sophie and me to stay in Westview. They'd save money if they helped us live in an apartment with an attendant to come help us every day."

"When am I going to meet Sophie?" Maria asks, looking at the picture on the wall above his bed. Sophie is a tiny woman with a pleasantly round face and the distinctive eyes of a person born with Downs Syndrome.

"Come to the People First meeting next week. She'll be there," Tommy says, his eyes gleaming. "When am I going to meet Randall?"

"That's private."

"Why is that private when everybody and his brother can tell Sophie and me what to do? You don't think our lives are as important as yours."

"How can you say that?"

"We're less of a priority. That's why I've been trying to get everyone in Westview out to vote. That's the only way anyone will hear us."

"I hear you, Brother," Maria says, *as if I have a choice.*

On a bookcase next to Tommy's bed is a picture of their mother and sculptures that he's molded from clay, semi-human figures with huge, blank eyes, horned heads, ghostly shapes resembling men but without feet or legs.

He reaches over and picks up a new glob of clay.

"What are you making?" Maria asks.

"Whatever shows up," Tommy says. "It is what it is. That's enough." His face glows as he works. A form appears. A god? A goddess? Like petroglyphs painted on ancient cave walls, the clay is Tommy's defiant statement: "I'm still here."

When Maria was in her teens, she used to pray that her brother would have an accident in his wheelchair. An elderly driver would have a heart attack and plow into the little creep as he rolled along the street. No one else would get hurt, but Tommy would die. She was five when Tommy was born, and the Farini family was caught up in a whirlwind within which Maria had disappeared. "Little Bird," her parents called her brother because his mouth was always open. Her mother always said she knew something wasn't right. Tommy was too limp. Slept too much. Gained more weight than the average baby. At two, he still couldn't walk, didn't smile. Maria tagged along as her parents ferried Tommy from pediatrician to neurologist in search of answers. When he did start walking, it was on tiptoe. Instead of falling down on his bottom like other babies, he stiffened and fell straight back. "Well, he'll never be a quarterback on the football team," one doctor said, scratching his head. Always Tommy was difficult to understand, words mumbled, speech rapid. Muscular dystrophy, the myotonic variety, an equal opportunity, no-gender preference variety. Painful spasming of muscles after exertion. A slowly progressive disease.

When Tommy was five and cherubic, he was chosen as

the March of Dimes poster child. A photographer flew to Denver from Los Angeles and decked him out in a sailor's suit. Tommy smiled gamely on the telethon, with all its glitz and schmaltz. He touched hearts and opened wallets. Shades of tin cups and Tiny Tim. Maudlin music was the backdrop to the myth that disabled people must be eternally dependent, childlike, in need of charity. To be pitied. That there was a cure out there somewhere in that vast audience. Give dollars, get miracles. From an early age, Maria learned how the world was divided into *us* and *them,* the lucky and the unlucky. Somehow Maria had landed in the realm of the lucky, although she's never felt lucky.

Now Tommy isn't cute anymore. No one is asking him to be a poster adult.

Last October, during the daily bustle of customers, Tina had given Maria a broad wink. "He's here again," Tina said.

"Who?" Maria asked, balancing a full tray on her right arm. The day had been busy because of the lasagna special.

"The man who has sat at one of your tables for the last month. Don't tell me you haven't noticed."

Randall needed at least a half-hour of air conditioning, two glasses of ice water before he ordered his steak, medium rare, Caesar salad.

"What do you do?" Maria asked Randall.

"I'm a telephone repairman," he said, wiping his forehead with a red handkerchief. They chatted about how hot it got up on the ladder, about all the electrolytes he lost. Maria left her phone number on the bill. Randall left a big tip and called her for a date.

Maria had stopped going to Confession because she knew she'd never be absolved when she kept repeating the sin. Eventually, she had stopped going to Mass too. She missed the cathedral with its carved doors, curved gold ceiling, stained-glass windows; the altar with its bronze Christ, mixture of incense, melting candle wax permeating everything.

The end of their affair started so slowly that Maria hadn't noticed at first. There was no argument, only shy loneliness. One day when they were shopping at the mall, they walked by a child with cerebral palsy and Randall said, "poor slob" under his breath. Maria knew then she would never introduce him to her brother. When they went dancing, they drank wine and watched the dancing couples and Maria wondered why she was here looking at his sweaty face.

Last week Randall sat at table 11 eating his steak when he said, "I'll be honest with you." Maria cringed because his honesty could be brutal. "You're a very nice woman, Maria," Randall began, "but I can't marry you." She had already known their relationship was over. What made Maria furious now was that Randall had sworn that he'd gotten himself fixed. The fact that he didn't want children was one of his most attractive qualities. Could this be a miraculous vasectomy reversal perhaps? "I'm shooting blanks," Randall had said soon after they met. But Maria carried proof inside her body that this was not true. What if her child had the same disability as her brother? What had she been thinking?

Special Needs is the term that has defined her brother's life. SSI. Medicaid. Physical supervision. Experts came and went and Maria lived on the edge of the chaos. Her mother was an overprotective Italian matriarch, not to mention religious. Very big with the saints. If Maria said "Mom, I flunked chemistry," she'd say, "Pray to St. Bartholomew."

"There's a saint who covers chemistry?"

"If you read your Bible, you'd know." Her mother only set out tomato plants when the moon was in the waning phase. She prayed over the arugula and zucchini. Voices rose through the radiator vents, those little cages Maria could look down and hear every word and shout.

"The doctors say Tommy would be better off in an institution," her father yelled.

"Over my dead body," her mother said.

"Is that what it's going to take?"

Many nights there were slamming doors. One night, when Maria was eleven, her father left and never came home again. Maria and her mother became equals, taking care of Tommy, planning meals, a quick run through the house with a sweeper, all done in a haphazard fashion.

Tommy always went crazy when it thundered and slept with a flashlight. She heard him blubbering at three in the morning. "What's the matter?" she yelled and then sat by his bed until he fell back asleep. When he was ten, Tommy underwent two spinal surgeries to prevent his body from collapsing in on itself. The first surgery winched his spine into a vertical posture and the second fused the bones to keep him upright. On the night before his operation, Maria held her mother's hand as Tommy asked the doctor, "Will I die?" "You might," the doctor said.

Tommy couldn't speak when he came out of recovery,

but by a prearranged signal, he blinked twice to tell them, "I'm all right."

Even now, so many years later, growing-up memories come at Maria like high-speed snapshots, all shapes and colors, rather than narrative continuity. Time. A series of conscious moments. The fields around their farmhouse went fallow, the pond at the back of the garden went dry. Their small home kept out snow and rain. They ate stewed chicken and homemade noodles on Sunday, took in a movie on Saturday afternoon. Their mother was big on ritual: Gregorian chants on the stereo over lingering meals, drinking cocoa as snow fell against windows. She gave Maria and Tommy long speeches about which perennials grew best in rocky Colorado soil: Ozark Sundrop, Prairie Dusk Penstemon, Allium Silver Spring. Maria is the perennial that keeps coming back year after year. Tommy is a hothouse flower, a constant reminder that all humans are vulnerable. As long as she could, her mother had bucked the prevailing expert thinking by keeping Tommy at home. Helping him on with his braces was a fact of life. Maria helped her brother get dressed, pulled up his pants, lifted him off the toilet, wiped him. That's just the way it was. The way Tommy scraped his teeth on his fork when he ate drove Maria crazy.

"Other families ship kids like Tommy off," Maria said during one heated argument. The scarred kitchen table was heaped with catalogs for organic vegetables. Garden tools lay on a chair.

"Don't ever talk that way again," her mother said. "Normals," Tommy called people like Maria. "Whitecoats," Tommy called his legion of doctors. Maria was sixteen when she was wheeling Tommy along the sidewalk in his wheelchair. A stranger stepped right in front of them, forcing Maria to bring the wheelchair to a screeching halt.

"If I were you, I'd kill myself," the woman hissed, her face level with Tommy's. It was all in the tone, as if the mere sight of Tommy was an offense, that he really should take the hint. The woman was gone before Maria or Tommy could respond. When they got home and told their mother, she sat calmly listening, as if she'd heard it all before.

"What gave that woman the right to think she could act that way, Mom?" Maria had asked.

"She spoke out of fear and ignorance. His disability is not who your brother is," their mother had said as she helped Tommy take off his braces. "Choose your own label, Tommy."

"I like the word 'cripple.' It's like a raised fist. 'Cripple' has soul-power."

Maria watched as her mother, in her old print dress and tennis shoes, played on the floor with Tommy, helped him learn to read, did endless range-of-motion exercises while Stravinsky's *The Firebird* filled the house. All those years her mother had nurtured a six-foot corn plant in the sunroom off the kitchen. The kids tore off leaves and their mother often forgot to water it, but as old leaves dropped off, fresh green leaves sprouted from its center. "Like our family," her mother had said, "plain, not at all exotic or even attractive, but surviving."

Driving the interstate, Maria curses Randall all the way to her appointment with the genetic counselor. Ms. Hewitt is heavyset with dark hair parted in the middle, a sixties flower child in a batik smock and sandals, transplanted into a new millennium. She talks with a lisp and a musical voice.

"Genetic counseling is really about prediction and statistical probabilities," she says as she hands Maria a cup of chamomile tea. "We're at a stage in our understanding of human genetics where almost everything has been promised—from immortality, to a cure for cancer, to the possibility of bringing all life processes under control. For instance, just a sample of your saliva on that cup could predict what you'll die of," Ms. Hewitt says. Maria feels the blood drain from her face. Warily, she sets the teacup back on the table, as if it were toxic.

"What can I do for you?" Ms. Hewitt asks gently.

"My brother has muscular dystrophy. I'm wondering if I carry the gene. If I have a child, will he have this disease too?" Maria's voice rises in pitch.

"Are you pregnant?"

"Yes. It wasn't planned."

"I understand. Here is a book I want you to read about genetic testing. When you come back next week, we can talk about it."

Ms. Hewitt tells Maria her options. Contraception (too late), sterilization (Randall tried and failed), abortion. The big "A." And finally Maria understands why her mother fought for Tommy's rights like a tigress. "Disability has always been a civil rights issue," Maria's mother always said. "The fact that Tommy has trouble finding a wheelchair-accessible bathroom is the same thing as when there were "white only" signs on restroom doors."

Later that night, Maria reads about the double helix, spiraling ladder, twin coil. The shorthand sign for life, science, the future. She reads how DNA has replaced

Newton's apple, Einstein's hair, the mushroom cloud of the hydrogen bomb as the most important scientific image in our culture. She reads how scientists have proven that all living things on the planet are related; that, at a distant moment in the past, we were all born together. The secret of life. The mighty gene as medical salvation.

Maria has a recurring dream: she's back home standing by the pond in the back yard as babies float by just below the surface. Dozens of them. They are alive but not struggling or trying to swim, looks of disbelief on their little faces. Babies, like they told her about in Sunday School—the ones who died before they could be baptized. Stuck in limbo on a technicality until the end of the world. And her mother is in the dream, alive again, walking towards her, holding out a baby that turns into Tommy, grown-up, but still a child.

The dining room is full of wheelchairs and loud chatter. Tommy is leading the monthly session of the People First Chapter at Westview. After one too many heavy doors slammed in his face, he became an activist. The day the Americans With Disability Act became law, Tommy zoomed around his room throwing confetti, shouting, "We're free!" Tommy is known for leading protests in front of buildings to force them to comply with the new law. "Down with barriers. No more stairs. No more heavy doors. No more curbs."

"This is my sister, Maria," Tommy says. "Meet Sophie."

"Nice to meet you," Sophie says.

"Likewise," Maria says, shaking her hand.

"Find a seat. We're going to start." Sophie pushes

Tommy's wheelchair closer to the table, leans down to kiss his cheek as she takes the seat next to him. Tommy beams and runs a finger timidly along Sophie's knee.

Maria sits at the table, tired eyes fixed on a space between her brother and the love of his life.

The meeting sets off on a rambling course. There is no set agenda, but everyone sitting around the table gets a chance to speak. Maria has heard it all before: moving out of Westview, jobs, improving the lighting and safety at the institution, ending the use of punishment by Westview staff, re-establishing ties with lost family members, relationships.

"My job is too boring. I don't make enough money," Paul says, a handsome man in his forties who came to Westview after a head injury.

"Tell the coordinator that you want a different job. Ask your parents to help," Tommy says.

"I want to take care of myself," Mark says.

"My sister can help you," Tommy says, pointing proudly at Maria. "She's very smart. She can find a lawyer maybe. Get your guardianship changed. Couldn't you, Maria?"

"Not this time, Tommy," Maria says, not able to look at him because of the disappointment she'll see.

"Why?"

"I don't have the time right now. I've got to sort out a lot of things," she says, rising to leave.

When her mother had complained of pain in her back, Maria had said, "It's because you lift Tommy in and out of the bathtub." "It's nothing," her mother told Maria, insisting that she was only tired and rundown and only had a cold the week before she was opened and closed on a surgical table at Denver General.

"The Holy Mother will heal me," she said after she received the diagnosis and was, once again, home in bed and resting after receiving chemo. Ovarian cancer. Already it was in her bones. She was in and out of the hospital for months, scanned, probed, plied with cancer-killing poison.

"It's not fair," Maria had said.

"Don't be bitter, honey. I accept it as God's will."

"God's will," Maria had snorted. But she'd grown up listening to her mother pray to St. Ann for rain, for the corn, and wheat, and barley, so of course He'd make her well.

Sun was just coming through the curtain. Her mother had been thrashing around, moaning, trying to yank off her oxygen mask. Then right when the sun hit her face, she quieted down, quit fighting. Maria leaned over and stroked her forehead. Her mother looked right at her. Maria was sure she felt her touch, heard when she said, "I love you. Thanks for all the sacrifices." Then Maria said the one thing she knew her mother wanted to hear: "I'll take care of him for you, Mom. Make sure he's safe. You can go now." She died less than an hour later.

From then on, it had been just Maria and Tommy, *as it was in the beginning, and ever shall be, world without end, amen,* just like their mother had prayed.

Maria is at work when she feels a rush of warm blood. She asks Tina to take over her tables and sits in the bathroom trying to stop it with toilet paper, tries to sit very still. She thinks maybe if she crosses her legs tightly enough, she can save her baby. A large clot passes and

Maria puts on a pad and feels as if she might pass out.

"Are you okay? You've been in there a long time," Tina calls. Maria is sitting on the floor next to the sink when Tina comes in.

"Better call an ambulance. I'm bleeding pretty bad," Maria says, two shades beyond ashen. As the ambulance speeds down Arapahoe, Maria focuses on how the light on top of the ambulance colors the raindrops red. In the ER, lights glare off white walls and bleaches out the face of the nurse who helps Maria onto the stretcher. She waits to feel relieved but is surprised at the grief welling up for this life that had ended before it began. For this child she will never hold.

When Maria gets back to her room after the D&C, Tina is waiting.

"You should have told us, Maria," Tina says softly. "Al would have given you longer breaks if he'd known that you were pregnant." Tears gather in Tina's eyes.

"I was worried that the baby might have muscular dystrophy too. I even went to see a genetic counselor. Maybe I caused my miscarriage."

"You have that much power? I don't think so."

"My mother spent her life taking care of my brother. I always swore I'd have a different kind of life. Tommy has gotten permission to live in an apartment with a woman he's in love with…. If they can't make it on their own, I'm the one who will have to fix things." Maria starts to cry. Tina sits on the edge of her bed, offers her a tissue.

"You have no control over your brother's illness or happiness. It's neither your responsibility nor your right to tell Tommy how to live his life."

"That's what my mom always said. Help me find my

clothes. They're letting me out of here."

Tina helps Maria on with her skirt and blouse, helps her check out of the hospital, drives her through the deepening dusk towards home.

After sixteen months of receiving bureaucratic shrugs and being told "your request is in the pipeline," Tommy is moving into his own place. A custom-built apartment with access to a large balcony with a view of the mountains. A kitchen fitted with appliances at wheelchair level. When Maria arrives to help him move, Westview residents are gathered, many in wheelchairs, in an alcove just off the foyer. Mark, a thin, dignified man, cradles a fiddle under his chin, looking dapper with a snowy beard, red suspenders. As he begins to play, tired bodies straighten, heads bob, hands clap. Sober faces break into smiles. Toes in slippers tap the floor. Voices join in. "Don't Fence Me In." "For He's A Jolly Good Fellow." Tommy and Sophie hold hands.

"We're proud of you," Diane, the Social Worker, says. Sophie starts to cry and Tommy pats her shoulder.

"Don't worry. Only one more week and we'll be together," he says.

With a chorus of farewells and good-luck wishes, Tommy wheels out of Westview. Maria drives her brother to his new apartment, past gray miles of strip malls. Past the Catholic school that Maria attended but kept Tommy out. Past the cemetery where their mother rests. She drives defensively against the terrors of the six-lane road.

"My own place." Tommy bounces on the seat in excitement. "You don't have to worry about Sophie and me. We'll be great. I feel okay with me. It's the rest of the world that has a problem. Everybody's got handicaps. Mine just show more than most. Even you have them."

"What? You mean your sister isn't perfect?" Maria laughs, bracing herself for the list that she knows is coming.

"Stubborn. Impulsive. But you make a perfect chocolate milkshake so that makes up for everything. All I want is to go to the same places you go. Like everybody else. Sophie and I are just a little strange, but nonviolent," Tommy says, giving Maria his special smile.

"Just like the people who come into the restaurant every day," Maria laughs.

She parks the car and pulls the new wheelchair out of the back seat. Tommy wheels past mothers and fathers on doorsteps. Girls stand in the shadows with their boyfriends. A large group of boys laugh and yell catcalls on the corner. Little girls play a singing game in the middle of the sidewalk. Boys run in and out, chasing each other, throwing balls, laughing, shouting.

Someone strikes up a dance tune on a street organ, and Tommy rolls into his new home humming along, jiggling his feet, free to taste the simple joy of deciding when to go to bed, when to rise, how he'll spend his day, whom he will love. And for Maria, being healthy and able to walk is miracle enough.

QUEEN OF THE SUGARHOUSE

From the hall, I hear Mama ordering the nurse: "Raise the window two inches. Don't put my suitcase on the top shelf. I can't reach it." Electronic sliding doors open and close. Workers in blue scrubs carrying machines, bags of blood, parade by. Doors go in and out like a breathing chest, and I sit helpless.

Mama is scheduled for six chemotherapy treatments, one series a month, all intravenous, in the hospital. "Try this vein," she orders the nurse, who has spent half an hour feeling her arms, putting a tourniquet on first her left, then her right. Finally, the needle rests in the crook of her arm, must be tied to a board so she won't forget and bend it. Hot flashes make her skin glow red, her face darken, sweat collect on skin. She's shrinking. A steel pole ticks, counts each drop as the yellow liquid begins its search-and-destroy mission. No turning back. An interesting torture this, watching my mother vomit bile. She's fidgety, can't stand to be touched. It's hard to stay long with Mama's pain.

She retches. As I ease her back onto the pillows, the gown flaps up and I see the red mark where her right breast used to be. "Why was it that Dr. Lenowitz called me, instead of you?"

"I didn't think you'd come. Denver is so far away. Do you ever wonder why people don't love each other more?"

"Don't start. You know why I left."

The nurse hurries in to check the IV. Mama's arm is puffy. Time to search for a new vein.

I tiptoe out, leaving the door ajar so I can hear if she calls. I walk up and down the corridor of Sugar Creek Hospital, with its fifty beds and mask of polished floors and papered feet, gleaming machinery, closed doors where scalpels part skin. That sharp, clean smell of disinfectant, the terror of a child with a broken arm. Shock trails in behind accident victims. Loved ones lie still and breathless in small rooms.

When I was little, we used to sit on the back porch when the Ohio night was clear and watch the stars. "There's the Big Dipper and Little Dipper and North Star," Mama had said.

Sometimes there were satellites moving through the stars. Sometimes a wolf howled. When I asked Mama if she were frightened of them when she collected maple syrup, she said, "They don't mean us any harm. I trust them more than people."

Maple sugaring was how we made our living. Spring came and we hung out the wooden buckets during the first spurt of warm weather. There was a clatter as Mama and I removed buckets, one by one, from the sled. Steam rose off the sweating backs of the horses. Nellie nuzzled Fred as if whispering encouragement. Mama stepped between them, adjusting their harness. "You poor slobs," she'd say as their wet hides rippled beneath her hands. Far down the hill, the sugarhouse appeared and disappeared in mist.

Mama was always handsome, and proud, and belligerent as she bartered jars of maple syrup for a brake job for our truck. Either she came out ahead on a deal, or she took revenge on the closest person around, who was always me. The winter I was sixteen she had an accident and broke her right leg. The limp made her outrageously demanding. "Have you fed the chickens yet? Fetch more wood for the sugar house." I used to cry whenever she tried to pull me onto her lap. Her touch could be a licking or a hug; I never knew which to expect. Even a treat, like popcorn or chocolate, could lead to appalling scenes, as if she'd forgotten how to give or receive pleasure. Somewhere during those growing-up years, Mama's bitterness was passed on to me, a family heirloom like the chipped Haviland china, the Star-of-Bethlehem quilt pulling apart at the seams.

I drive Mama in for her doctor's appointment a week after she finishes with the last chemo treatment. She is still in the examination room putting on her clothes when Dr. Lenowitz turns to me and asks, "How much should I tell her, Sue?"

"Tell her the truth," I say. Lenowitz clutches Mama's chart and walks to where she's sitting.

"I'm sorry, Cora, but the last pathology report wasn't as good as I'd hoped. There were cancer cells in three of the lymph node biopsies we took. The microscope doesn't lie." His voice trails off as Mama shakes her head. From the tight pursing of her lips, her rigid back, I know she's furious. "There's still some chance for a cure if you're willing to do six more weeks of chemo and radiation," Lenowitz adds.

"We'll let you know," I say as I help Mama with her coat. We drive in silence back to the farm. How golden a day it is, the valley strewn with maple leaves, the sky a featureless white. Green, brown, gold coins float down from the trees in front of the truck. The water in the creek is shallow. Almost dusk. Wind picks up. Someone is mowing late October grass, a final shearing before snow falls. This is the time of year when anything can happen: eighty-degree sunscreen weather or a blizzard. *Be prepared, mittens, winter coat, boots*, Mama had taught me. The evening sky is so pure it catches me in the throat.

"Why didn't I notice how beautiful Silver Creek was when I was growing up?" I ask.

"You were too busy getting out of here," Mama says as she leans on my arm, short of breath. "I always knew you'd leave."

"I'm here now."

"Yes," Mama whispers. The woods in the back of the house are full of fire. Wind escapes its den. Mallards nibble frantically on the lawn.

First light slants through the maple grove. Swing feet down, feel for slippers, floor slick with frost. Jeans, red flannel shirt. This farmhouse, gray from where paint has worn off and never been replaced. Iron-red water runs through the tap. Shuffle to the kitchen. There's only room for one person to move. Scramble eggs. Add a little milk, whisk the fork around the bowl so there will be no white strings. Daub butter on rye bread. Boil water for peppermint tea. Arrange orange slices, like a daisy on the plate.

Her door is ajar and I kick it with my foot. She's sitting in the rocker, her head laid back, hair spread out like seaweed. Clumps of grey cling to the doily, parts of her falling away. Soon she'll be bald. She smiles as I hand her the tray.

"I don't know if I can eat anything. But it looks so pretty," she says. The tray wobbles in her hands. I steady it just in time.

"Try something," I suggest. A piece of bread falls into her lap. Her face glows with sweat. Her fork slides across the plate and nestles against a clump of egg.

"I feel like I'm being nibbled to death by sharks," she says as the fork slides from her hand. "Help me back to bed." I half carry her, tuck in the quilt. Already she's asleep. Through the window I hear the chatter of Sugar Creek as water ricochets off rocks, water flows so close to the house.

When I had said that I wanted to be a nurse, Mama had laughed. "You, who can't stand to watch when I butcher pigs?" I protested, "Nursing is different." Now I am my mother's nurse, emptying the foul emesis basin, checking her biopsy dressings for drainage, carefully noting the time I give her medications, the way Dr. Lenowitz instructed.

Nursing is like tapping maples. You have to be sensitive to when the time is right, know when to stop. After I give her a back rub, pain lines around her eyes evaporate. I become expert at slipping bits of morphine through tubing. I learn how to sit quietly, without having to give Mama anything, without having to take anything away for myself.

One afternoon I think Mama is asleep, but when I turn from folding laundry, her eyes plead. "Tell me about your life in Denver. Is there a man?" she whispers. I say nothing. With all her scars and bruised arms and stooped back, this is not the same woman who slapped me, forced me to work long hours in the fields. That was the woman I always feared, not this ruin.

After I tuck Mama in, I sit on the porch. A strong breeze sweeps into the slim upper branches of maples, stirs leaves to a frenzy, fades, reappears twirling dead leaves onto the driveway. For this moment, there's no pattern to things, no scheme. Wind spins off the trees, hissing, nagging, repeating its grudges. Somewhere a tractor groans up a long hill.

"People in this town can't be trusted," she used to tell me. "What did they ever do to you, Mama?" I would ask. In Sugar Creek, six months can become six years with the deceptive ease of a film dissolve. Old-fashioned trick shot. A one-way street runs around the square. All cars park parallel. The tiny hospital is always in danger of closing. No hospice. No visiting nurses. I grew up in the middle of nowhere, an Ohio countryside so lonely that even stones seemed lost. Walking is measured by hours instead of blocks. Foreclosure circles like a buzzard. Barbed wire cuts farms into lots and pens. The medicine of choice is stomping feet soles at Grange dances, booze, winter frolics between sheets. God is sun, rain, a prevailing wind moving across shaded windows, and maple sugar gleaming in a jar.

I worked alongside Mama that hot summer I was eleven, slapping paste on the dining- room walls. Rolls of paper. Cans of glue. Knives, brushes were piled into a basket. She wallpapered our living room with a floral pattern that had more than a touch of purple. For months we couldn't eat in that room because it was stacked with wallpaper rolls. *Why can't she be neat just once, remember to smooth out the sheets?* But Mama had done the job when the spirit moved her, humming the whole time. I hated her for not caring enough to make our house look like everyone else's.

"Someday you'll be a great wallpaper woman too," Mama said while I watched. Not one of my life goals. Mama worked with tremendous energy. Hot afternoons, she rolled up her sleeves and I saw her sinewy arms.

"Why are you doing this?"

No answer. Mama turned on the radio, and her body swayed to the high notes of Ella Fitzgerald, *How High The Moon.* At the end of the day, she sat lotus-legged in front of a newly blooming wall, nodded and smiled, rocking back and forth in delight.

The phone lies dead in my hand. The floor lamp casts its pallor onto the blue and red rug in the middle of the floor, bleeding into one dark cloud. Nothing more can be done to treat my mother, Lenowitz said, neither chemo nor radiation until she regains some appetite and strength. Mama's life no longer has a rhythm, only a regimen. Medications. Dressing changes.

Bath. Up on the commode. Cancer is that lonely place where even a daughter cannot follow. A month after she came off all medications, Mama's hair grows back, thick and spiky and white instead of gray. Fungus on her esophagus and stomach ulcers make meals horrors. She lives on a fortified drink, mixed with chocolate ice cream that I make three times a day. Nothing tastes like it should.

I turn Mama over in bed, prop her back against a pillow. "I had such a strange, wonderful dream," she says. "I flew over the house with a full head of hair. Time is rushing. I don't want anything to rush past me anymore. I read about this preacher. He and his wife swallowed overdoses of sleeping pills." Her cheeks are flushed against the pillowcase. "They left a letter saying they'd been planning it for a long time. Would you help me, Sue?"

I tuck in her quilt, pretend I haven't heard. Slowly Mama closes her eyes. After shutting the bedroom door, I go into the garden to pick lettuce for dinner. Memories of all those summers I spent pulling weeds rush back. All around, there is a thick honey stillness. Zucchini and tomatoes and lima beans line up in neat rows. Cantaloupe threatens to run over everything. Vines leapfrog over radishes and carrots. I hear a small sound and turn to see a robin caught in the net trellis which holds up the snap peas. The bird lies very still, one wing outspread. I take the kitchen knife out of my apron and cut away the twine until the robin is able to soar free.

When I was little, Mama used to joke that even church mice wouldn't live in our house. Being poor never seemed funny to me. There was no humor in having holes in the bottoms of my shoes or being the only kid in the class not to have money for assembly. Poverty meant my mother could blow up when I asked for a nickel, her voice harsh, accusatory. Mama worked at the kitchen table cutting covers for my schoolbooks out of grocery bags. Anything to save a dollar. While other kids went roller skating or to the circus, I followed Mama between rows of sweet corn and maple trees. The only visitors who knocked on our door were salesmen and bill collectors. From an early age I was the one who dealt with them because of Mama's temper. I was pounding spouts in maple trees, emptying sugar buckets, firing up the furnace while my classmates were hanging out at the drugstore, jitterbugging in the school gymnasium, filling out college applications.

Mama was queen of the sugarhouse. How she reveled in the roar she created. The old sugarhouse stood on the edge of Miller Swamp. It was a small, rectangular wooden building with boards hanging loose on the sides and a roof in none-too-good condition. There were no windows, only a large solid swinging door at one side and two holes cut just below the peak of the roof at each end, allowing steam to escape. In winter, the floor became a sheet of ice. Always there was the danger of burning embers escaping the timber box, igniting walls.

It all came crashing down in the spring I turned sixteen. I had gone to bed early. Mama said she had to get the furnace going for our sugaring the next morning. Sometime during the night I awoke to shrieks and obscenities interspersed with deep racking sobs. From the back porch, I saw embers shooting out of the chimney of the sugarhouse. I pulled on my jeans, and raced across flat frozen earth, down into the shadowed valley, the last place that light visits.

Mama, in her torn jeans and grey sweater, sat with one hand on her head and one hand holding a whiskey jar. She had lit the arch. The evaporator roared as steam shot up from boiling sap. The power of fire shifted coals, stirred wood. The whole sugarhouse was so dense with fog that I could see no further than a few feet. "Is anyone there?" Mama's voice boomed. The roof ignited. A falling rafter caught Mama in her right leg. I pulled her out just before the roof caved in.

She sleeps most of every day. Night is day. Day is night. She rarely speaks. Her arms and legs are as thin as a boat person's. I hold the glass while she sips juice through a straw to make the paste needed to get pills down. Two, three times a day, I empty the catheter bag, flushing away her will to hang on. Medications, bed-bath, onto the commode. I give her a back rub. I slide a bit of morphine through tubing.

Pain fills my mother, like water filling a syringe. I fantasize about slipping into her room while she naps, leaning my weight and strength on a pillow, then restoring the scene to normal. No one would ever know. I'm the only one she has.

Days are a game of shutting everything out except helping with Mama's catheter and bedpan, cleaning mucus from her lips and eyes. Her organs are giving up. Washcloth to ashen skin that threatens to fall inward like dry wood. Even washing my own hands with green soap can't remove the smell.

All through high school Mama patrolled the phone. Our worst fight was when I was talking to Tom and Mama pulled the phone's plug. I became an expert at lying. *I was in the library. Beth loaned me this sweater,* I said when I was really sleeping with Tom and I'd stolen the sweater from Sears. The summer before my eighteenth birthday, I followed Tom to Denver and got a job as a bank clerk. Two months later, Tom left after he fell in love with a bartender at Miller's Bar. It took six months for me to call home.

"You'll never make it on your own."

"And there's so much opportunity in Sugar Creek?"

"You're just like your father."

"At least we had sense enough to leave," I said just before I slammed down the phone.

He left before I was born. Someone at school told me he died when an oil rig caught fire. All Mama would ever say about my father was "that loser," her voice trailing off like a scratch mark on skin.

I move a cot into the corner of Mama's bedroom. She sleeps, her head back, mouth slack, hardly rippling the sheets. White hair, wan skin crumbles into desert parchment. I could encircle her upper arm with a thumb and forefinger if I wanted.

"Oh," she says, opening her eyes to slits. "You're here. Have you had lunch?"

"Don't worry. I'll eat."

"I'm always so tired." Her eyes close again. Long after I think she's asleep, Mama whispers. "No needles. No hospitals. Promise me." She floats far out on an island of morphine, drifts on her small disintegrating raft. No way to row back. Alone on her white narcotic beach almost free of the enemy that never sleeps.

In the backyard, crickets have started their song. Some evenings the sky looks cobalt blue, bewildered, questioning, and other times magenta, as if impatient for night to settle in. Tonight the sky makes all my senses sharper, as if I were waiting for something huge.

When I check on Mama, she's sleeping on her side, just

as I left her, shriveled and still, like a monkey in a cage. There is a whistling sound in her throat, her breathing wet, as if her lungs were being rained on. I pick up the morphine vial on the bedside stand. "Keep her comfortable," Dr. Lenowitz had instructed. How easy it would be to open the vial, slip in the syringe, give her the whole vial instead of a fraction. My hands shake as I pick up the vial, turn it over and over in my hands. Quietly I set it back down on the table.

Gradually Mama gains enough strength to sit in the chair again. She keeps food down. She is strong enough to sit on the porch, to walk to the mailbox at the end of the driveway. Lenowitz wants to try one more round of chemo. "There's a new experimental drug that we can try."

"Let me talk to her," I say. Mama sits on the edge of the bed rubbing her bad leg. Her gown is up around her belly. Thin legs sway. "Lenowitz just called. He wants you to try a new drug. What do you think?"

"I told you. No more hospitals. No more chemo. Can't anyone hear me?"

Mama actually gains five pounds, once again looks forward to real food from the garden: zucchini, ripe melons, melt-in-your-mouth sweet corn. A couple of days later we make a mad escape from bruised veins and medications for pain. The darkness of the Rialto Theater is a twilight reverie. Mama relaxes, slides down in her seat, her spirit free. The dancing cone of light bounces off her white head, lined face. We sit hypnotized by sound, music, words dancing on a long stem of light. *Terms Of Endearment* is playing, a movie that balances between funny and sad, moments of truth and moments of absurdity, a lot like life. Mama and I are up there on the screen, except it's the mother who is dying instead of the daughter. For two hours, only fantasy is real.

As I guide Mama out of the almost empty theater, we both are dazed, wrapped up in the story we've just seen, feeling the cold. "Sleepy, Mama?" Her body is soft, limp, as if she were emerging from hypnosis.

"Am I like that mother in the movie? That domineering?"

"You never let me bring anyone to our house. Why?" With difficulty, I help Mama get comfortable, fasten her seatbelt. I start the truck and back out of the parking spot in front of the theater.

"They might steal us blind." Every word ends with a question mark, as if her life has become unbelievable.

"What do we have that anyone would want to steal?"

I drive towards home, taking the shortcut through Slocum Woods instead of the interstate. "All I knew when I was growing up was there was something wrong with me. Everything was either black or white. No in-between. When I was in high school, if you didn't like my conversations, I'd hear the dial tone. You never trusted me. Why were you so angry all the time?"

"There was so much I wanted to do," Mama says. "I dreamed about robbing the Sugar Creek Bank so I wouldn't have to lug buckets of maple syrup. Traveling to Greece or Egypt. Buying a red car."

I park in front of our farmhouse and hold Mama up as we walk into the living room, with its cold fireplace and threadbare rug, and Currier-and-Ives prints on the wall.

"You don't have to do it, you know." She's short of breath from exertion but her words are clear.

"Who would take care of you if I didn't?"

"I saw you in my room that night. You picked up the vial of morphine and held it a long time. People usually fall away from somebody with cancer, but it's brought you home," Mama says.

As I walk to her side, she pulls me down onto the couch beside her, and tells me how, as a Depression child, she used to wake up hearing the sound of *Rags, Bottles, Sacks.* She heard the old man's cry long before she saw the tired, sway-backed horse with his load, his eyes large with pain, ribs showing.

She tells me how she'd met my father when he'd hired on for making maple syrup. He was moving, always moving, fleeing police. Maybe a new state, a new job would quiet his nerves, give him, at long last, the peace he was looking for. There were always ghosts to be fled, shadows who visited, noises that meant danger was gaining on him. A midnight departure was the only way he knew how to wipe the slate clean. Mama encloses me in her arms, and we rock back and forth, as if I were four, and she were well.

Winter is finally over. Spring shows herself in faint, indefinable signs: a warmer sun, geese honking overhead, a softening of snow crust into slush. Spring was when Mama used to bore holes in maples, insert metal spouts, hang wooden buckets. Juice wept from the maples' incisions.

Bathe her. Wash her hair. Rub her body with fine lotion. Feed ice chips. Stroke her hair, hands, forehead. Mama's restlessness weighs on me like a rock I can't lay down. Water glasses slip from my hands and break. Every day I think: *She can't get any worse*. After many calls, Lenowitz installs a morphine drip. I assist him as he puts in a needle with a plug just under Mama's clavicle. I wince every time Lenowitz tries, until the needle finally hooks skin. Mama's face screws up, as if she were crying, but no sound comes out. As Lenowitz shoots blood back into her neck, the blood is pale, not the deep red it once was. Lenowitz sets up the drip, the bag of glucose and morphine on a mechanical tree that holds the pump. He shows me how to operate it, how to mix the formula, the shot of Heparin to keep her vein open. In my nervousness, I prick my finger. I try again and get it right.

"She'll be comfortable now," Lenowitz says. "I'll check in often." He takes his coat and leaves. Mama is sleeping, her face a full moon hung in a starless sky. Death is a subtle whittling away of function and strength, as slow as an IV drip into a tired vein. As unglamorous as day- old bread.

Around three in the morning, I'm suddenly wide awake. I strain to detect any sound or movement from Mama only a few feet away. It is silence that awoke me. I can't bring myself to turn on a light for the longest time. No angels. No light. Mama left as instantly as a balloon flying out of an opened hand.

I bathe her, put on a clean nightgown. When I disconnect the IV tubing from her chest, I glance at the bag of fluid hanging on the IVAC. The door that holds the tubing is open, the bag empty, and I know that Mama cut herself out of the net.

Lenowitz arrives and listens with his stethoscope, checks her pupils with his little flashlight. "I found her when I woke up this morning. I slept on this cot."

"Yes," he says, glancing at the empty IV and back at

Mama lying so peacefully in her clean nightgown. "I'll have Schmidt's come get her, when you're ready." He pats my shoulder as he leaves. "Your mother was a very stubborn woman."

"Once she made up her mind, there was nothing anyone could do."

Suddenly the small house is full of neighbors who used to make fun of my mother, full of confusion, and prattle and work boots clomping on bare floors. All the men and women with whom Mama fought over property lines now come armed with roses, proverbs, casseroles, meat loaf, homemade bread. I don't own a black dress to wear to the funeral, and my mind clings to this problem like a crutch. White blouse and denim skirt will have to do.

Mama's closed casket rests at the foot of the altar of the Baptist Church that she never attended. White-gloved church ladies pour glasses of water, set up folding chairs, wave away mosquitoes with paper fans. The chapel is full and very quiet. I see faces I haven't seen since childhood, all my mother's enemies, one-time friends. As chapel bells chime, everyone looks dark and solemn, as if everyone knew this was how Mama would end up.

It has become sugar weather when no one was looking, that moment when sun and frost begin their contest, a see-saw, as sun draws sap up, and frost draws it down. Along the creek, shadows are long and dampness never leaves. Cottonwoods and poplars, straight and tall, reach towards light. I sit on my favorite rock, granite, scalloped with veins of ironstone, that I used to sit on when I was hiding from Mama. The scent of pine hovers. Wind riffles leaves.

Crows overhead cry, *amen, amen.* Water rustles over loose stones. Splashing water has all the time in the world to get where it's going. I think I hear Mama's voice, then realize it's only the sound of water over rocks. Tears are this river carrying me forward.

Acknowledgements

Grateful acknowledgment is given to the Editors of the following publications in which these stories have appeared:

"Mercy," *Intensive Care: More Poetry and Prose By Nurses,* (anthology), University of Iowa Press, 2003, Cortney Davis and Judy Schaefer, Editors.

"Think Beauty," *Westview: A Journal of Western Oklahoma,* Vol. 23, No. 1, (Fall, Winter), 2003), Fred Alsberg, Editor.

"Shift," *Georgia State University Review*, 2003, Katie Chaple, Editor.

"The Isolation Room," *Crucible* (40th Anniversary Issue) Vol.40, (Fall, 2004), Terrence L. Grimes, Editor.

"Testament" (an earlier version) appeared in *Ascent,* 1990, Audrey Curley, Editor.

"Queen of the Sugarhouse," *Thin Air Magazine,* Vol. VII, No. 1 (Issue 12), 2003, Charla Grenz, Editor.

I am grateful for the support for my writing given to me by Hedgebrook Cottages, the Ucross Foundation, the Rocky Mountain Women's Institute, the Arts and Humanities Assembly of Boulder, the Katherine Sharp Rachlis Memorial grant from the Ludwig Vogelstein Foundation, New York, and the Neodata Foundation.

About Atmosphere Press

Atmosphere Press is an independent, full-service publisher for excellent books in all genres and for all audiences. Learn more about what we do at atmospherepress.com.

We encourage you to check out some of Atmosphere's latest releases, which are available at Amazon.com and via order from your local bookstore:

Comfrey, Wyoming: Birds of a Feather, a novel by Daphne Birkmyer
Relatively Painless, short stories by Dylan Brody
Nate's New Age, a novel by Michael Hanson
The Size of the Moon, a novel by E.J. Michaels
The Red Castle, a novel by Noah Verhoeff
American Genes, a novel by Kirby Nielsen
Newer Testaments, a novel by Philip Brunetti
All Things in Time, a novel by Sue Buyer
Hobson's Mischief, a novel by Caitlin Decatur
The Black-Marketer's Daughter, a novel by Suman Mallick
The Farthing Quest, a novel by Casey Bruce
This Side of Babylon, a novel by James Stoia
Within the Gray, a novel by Jenna Ashlyn
Where No Man Pursueth, a novel by Micheal E. Jimerson
Here's Waldo, a novel by Nick Olson
Tales of Little Egypt, a historical novel by James Gilbert
For a Better Life, a novel by Julia Reid Galosy
The Hidden Life, a novel by Robert Castle
Big Beasts, a novel by Patrick Scott
Whose Mary Kate, a novel by Jane Leclere Doyle

About the Author

Constance Studer earned a MA in Creative Writing from the University of Colorado, Boulder. She draws from her twenty-years of experience as a registered nurse in her book, *Queen of the Sugarhouse*. She has enjoyed writer's residencies from the Rocky Mountain Women's Institute, the Ucross Foundation and Hedgebrook. She has received writing grants from the Arts and Humanities Assembly of Boulder, the Ludwig Vogelstein Foundation and the Neodata Endowment for the Arts and Humanities.

CPSIA information can be obtained
at www.ICGtesting.com
Printed in the USA
FSHW010209010921
84358FS